Angst of the Middle-School Newbie

Vol 1 :

The Philippians 4:13 Series

K L Dierking

DEDICATION

To my children

Jathe Alex Wampler

Mikayla Marie Wampler

Colby Marshall Wampler

Channing Elizabeth-Grace Dierking

I love you all the way around the world two times and back again.

Thank you for being my inspiration.

To Nolan, thank you for letting me follow my dreams.

I love you more every day.

To my Mom and Dad, Russ and Cheryl,

thank you for being the parents I've always hoped for.

I love you both so much.

THE ANGST OF THE MIDDLE-SCHOOL NEWBIE

~ 1 ~

Dear, Jesus, it's me ... Philippian Macedon from 222 Carthage Road. I don't know if You remember me or not. I haven't talked to You in a very long time but I visit Your house every single Sunday and most Wednesday nights for youth group. Mama says it's important for us to spend time with other people who love You, too.

Anyway, Jesus, today is my first day at my new school. Not my first day ever, but my first day in middle school. I'm the only one in my whole neighborhood going to sixth grade. My mom says the new school will be super fun, but I'm not sure. I'm scared I won't have any friends. Anyway, I guess I gotta go for now, since it's almost time to leave. Could You not let them laugh at me today, Jesus? Please? Just for today? Oh, and if You know where my dad is and if he talks to You today, could You please tell him I love him all the way around the world two times and back again? And that I miss him so much. Thank You, and Amen.

"Philip!" Mom called me to come to the kitchen. She's the only one allowed to call me 'Philip'. I don't normally like that name at all, but I don't mind it too much when she says it. I smelled the bacon Mom was frying as soon as I entered the hallway. My favorite. Well, that and scrambled eggs. Today being a special day and all, Mom said she would make my absolute favorite. Otherwise it would be Fruity Pebbles or Cheerios.

"Breakfast is almost ready. Get your plate." Mom nodded towards the cabinet with the plates in it, since both of her hands were busy cooking.

"I can't, Mom." I rubbed my belly with one hand and shoved a finger from my other hand halfway down my throat. Not enough to throw up but ... well, almost because that's how I was feeling. My stomach felt like the inside of a washing machine, twisting and turning super-fast. "I'm too scared to eat this morning, Mom. It might come back up if I do," I said.

Mom looked away with her head hanging. I had upset her and she was sad. Not as sad as she did the day Dad left in his uniform, but almost as sad. "Just try," she asked. She held the plate of warm bacon out so I could see all her hard work.

Jared, my mean big brother, jumped up and snatched my bacon. He shoved three whole pieces down his big mouth and swallowed them in one gulp ... without even chewing them first. He is the meanest, biggest brother anyone could have.

"Jared!" Mom yelled. She squinted her eyes, making them really small, and wrinkled her nose. That's her mad face.

"Not like he was going to be able to reach the plate anyway," Jared said. He crammed one of his thumbs into each of his ears and wiggled them in the air, while sticking his tongue out at me.

"Stop picking on your brother," Mom told him.

"Oh, come on, Mom." Jared plopped down in his seat at the kitchen table and took even more bacon from the plate Mom had put in the center for everyone. "Look how short he is. He's never going to be able to reach a plate." And then he laughed the way he always does. He laughed so hard he had to wrap his arms around his waist to keep his sides from hurting. He laughed so hard tears came out of both eyes like he was crying. Except he wasn't.

Most days I don't like my big brother, though Mom tells me someday we will be great friends. I doubt it. Mom never had a brother like Jared, so I don't think she knows what she's talking about. We are never going to be friends. Never!

"I grew a whole inch this summer, for your information," I told Jared. I bet he didn't know I measured myself every night. My mom hung a measuring chart on the inside of my closet door just so I could see I was growing. And I did! An entire inch! Shows how much Jared knows.

Jared chugged down the half-gallon of orange juice at once, all on his own, without sharing with me or Mom. Some of it ran out of his big mouth onto his shirt. He wiped his mouth with the back of his hand and put the empty container back on the table. "You're still going to be the shortest person in the whole school," he said. Then he started laughing all over again.

It was no use. I bet Jared was right. I've been the shortest person I've ever known for my whole life. And I am almost twelve years old. That's a very long time to be the shortest person in the world. Even if Mom says I am much smarter than most, I'm still the shortest.

I'm much shorter than all the other kids in the neighborhood. Most of them are as big as Jared, and they all like to pick on me because of it. I'm also the only kid in the neighborhood who wears glasses ... and mine are big and square. I didn't like them at first, but I do now. They are different. Mom says they're unique and that makes them special, just like me. The other kids don't think so. They think my glasses are funny-looking, and they laugh at me every time they see me wearing them, which is all the time since I can't see a thing without them.

"Got all your stuff in your fanny-pack there, Philly-Willy?" Jared balled up both fists and twisted them in his eyes. "Waah, waah, waah," he said, making cry-baby sounds.

"My name's not Philly-Willy and it's not a fanny-pack. It's a survival-pack." I crossed my arms over my chest and gave him the stink-eye. That's when I try to make the same mean face Mom makes. Now he knows I mean business and I'm not taking his name-calling any more.

"Don't forget your flashlight and whistle. The sun might burn out and you'll be all alone in the dark. Bet you'll be scared then, won't you?" he teased. "And take your inhaler, 'cause you know what happens when you get scared!"

I wish Dad was here. He's the only one who understands me. The only guy who doesn't pick on me, even when I get scared. He says he understands how I feel because he was the shortest person in his neighborhood too, and everyone picked on him. No one picks on him anymore since he's a Marine. He's the toughest guy I know. The toughest guy in the whole world.

"You guys better get moving." Mom pointed out the window. "The other kids are already leaving. You don't want to be late."

Jared ran out the door before me and hopped onto his bike before I could even get out the door. He has a black bike with a really cool light between the handlebars so he can ride at night with his friends. Mom only lets them ride on our road, but that's more than I get to do. Besides, I got stuck with a girl's bike; a really big pink girl's bike with a flowery basket on the front.

"It's all we can find right now for the money we have," Mom said the day she bought it at a consignment shop. She promised I'll get a new one for my twelfth birthday. Three more months. I know because I have it circled on the calendar, and every day I mark off another day. I can't wait. I'll get a boy's bike and it will be cooler than Jared's.

Sweat poured from the top of my head when I tried picking my gigantic girl's bike up so I could get onto it. The other kids flew past me, and dust flew all over my glasses. I wiped them with the bottom of my shirt and got onto my bike. I peddled as fast as I could to catch up with the others but I still got there last. By the time I made it to school and chained up my bike, I stank so much from sweating I had to go straight to the bathroom to wash my armpits.

Remind yourself to ask Mom about some deodorant tonight. You're old enough ... and you stink, I told myself. *It's definitely time for deodorant.*

The bell rang. *Great! Late on my first day! Ugh.*

~ 2 ~

"You must be Philippian Macedon." I hadn't been in class more than ten seconds before I was already getting yelled at by the teacher. I'm pretty sure she's a mom. She has that same mad look Mom gets. She pointed at the clock when she looked at me. "You're late!"

"I kn ... kn ... know." I stuttered. Ugh. I hate it when I stutter, but it happens whenever I have to speak in public, and especially when I'm nervous. "I had t ... t ... to go to the ba ... ba ... bathroom."

he whole class pointed at me and laughed. Already. My glasses slid down my nose. I pushed them back up and looked around the room. No other student had glasses. Not one.

Why me, Jesus?

I sat at the only empty desk in the room. I knew it was mine because there was a long piece of paper folded in half, standing up to make a name plate. It had "Phillipian Macedon" written on both sides. It was misspelled, as usual, but it was my name. The teacher stood at the front of the class, with her arms folded in front of her. The announcements were being read through the loud speaker hanging on the wall above the blackboard and we were supposed to be silent until they were finished.

This was my chance to scan the room and check out all the other kids in class. Certainly someone would be shorter than me, but I wouldn't know until everyone was standing.

Thirty-two students in all. Eighteen boys. Fourteen girls. None with glasses, besides me. Not one. Most of the boys had the same haircut. Short and way above their ears. Mine was longer. Shaggy, my mom called it. Sometimes it gets in my face and covers up my glasses, but I don't mind really.

The announcements came to an end and it was time for the Pledge of Allegiance. We all stood and faced the flag. One hand on our heart. I know I'm not supposed to, but I had to do it. I scanned the room while everyone was standing to see if anyone was shorter than me. At least the boys. Nope. It's me. I am the shortest. Again.

I wanted to sink in my chair when we finished the Pledge of Allegiance. I wanted to hide behind my book or something. Anything to keep from being noticed. If only I could become invisible.

The teacher cleared her throat really loud. She sounded the way my dad did when he had bronchitis and tried to clear his throat first thing every morning. She looked kind of like him, too - hair so short she could be a Marine like my dad. "I'm Mrs. Blueberry," she said. And she was serious. She didn't even crack a smile.

"Blueberry," one boy yelled. He pointed his finger at her and laughed so hard most of the class laughed with him. I don't know what was so funny, really. It's just a name, and there's nothing funny about a blueberry.

She looked over the rims of the glasses clinging to the tip of her nose. She raised her eyebrows and a million wrinkles covered her forehead. I knew that boy was in trouble.

"So ..." Mrs. Blueberry took a long pause as she walked towards the boy, with her arms folded in front of her again. She let her glasses fall around her neck from a long silver chain. She must not need them to see the way I do.

"Mister Boyette?" She put both of her hands down on his desk, and leaned close to his face. He wasn't laughing anymore, and the whole room was super quiet. "Am I going to have trouble out of you this year, Mr. Brian Boyette" she asked.

Brian Boyette didn't say anything. I think he was too afraid. I would be. He shook his head. Mrs. Blueberry waited a few seconds before taking her hands off his desk. His face was bright red, and it stayed that way for a really long time.

"Now, class, these are your assignments for the week. Write them down." She turned her back to the class and scribbled on the blackboard for several minutes.

"Your first homework assignment is due tomorrow."

"Tomorrow," she said again. "No excuses. I won't take it if it's late, and you will get a big fat goose egg for a grade. Write this down in your agendas. You'll each find one in your desk." No one had warned me about her. Not any of the kids in our neighborhood. Not one. She has to be the meanest teacher in the whole school. She's definitely the meanest teacher I have ever had. I took out my agenda like she said, and wrote down the assignment exactly the way she had it written on the board. I was too afraid not to.

Dear Jesus, it's me, Philippian Macedon from 222 Carthage Road. Well, not right now. Right now I'm at my first day of New Century Middle School. I hope You can hear me. I can't talk to You out loud right now but I have a big problem. I have a really mean teacher. I hope the rest of my teachers aren't like this. I don't know if You can, but my science teacher ... can you made her nicer? Please? I don't want two mean teachers in a row. Please, Jesus. Thank You, and Amen.

The rest of the class went by like a turtle running a marathon. I didn't hear much of what Mrs. Blueberry said. I was too busy looking around the room at the other kids. *Which one is going to end up being my best friend*, as Mom had promised. None of them looked particularly friendly, but I suppose they could have been too afraid, as I was, to even smile while in Mrs. Blueberry's class. The girls looked a lot friendlier. They were all sitting up straight, and most of them had long hair that went almost all the way down their back. *Maybe I can be friends with some of them.*

~ *3* ~

When the bell rang to change classes, I stepped into the hallway, hoping for some semblance of order. Signs maybe. Anything pointing me in the right direction or perhaps a Hall Monitor to show the way ... like my last school. There were none. Just a bunch of wild rabid animals bulldozing through the halls, as if they would evaporate into a pile of sawdust if they didn't make it to class on time.

Through the process of deduction, I managed to make it to science class just before the bell.

"Take a seat over there," the teacher pointed.

There she was. She was the prettiest girl I had ever seen. She had three little freckles on each cheek and shiny black hair. It was a strange but beautiful combination. Her hair was so long it touched her butt. She smiled at me when I sat next to her. Since ours were the only two seats at the table, I was pretty sure that meant she was going to be my science partner. I sure hoped so.

The two girls at the table next to ours must have been friends for a long time. Like maybe their whole lives. They were whispering and pointing at some of the other kids in the class, then at me.

"Hi, I'm Elizabeth Faith-Grace Winkworth," my science partner said. I had never met someone with such a long name before. She extended her hand for me to shake. Adults were the only people who had ever shaken my hand before. Never another kid like me. I shook her hand and smiled.

"Hi, I'm Philippian Mmm ... mmm ... Macedon."

"You must be from a different neighborhood than mine," she said. "I've never seen you before," she said, not even noticing my stutter. All her teeth sparkled when she spoke to me. *She spoke to me.* I could hardly believe it.

"I guess."

She pointed to my survival pack and smiled again. "I like camo," she said. "Whatcha got in it?"

My hands dripped with sweat. My heart pounded with such strength in my chest, I felt it in the back of my throat. My tongue grew thick like a sponge sucking in all the moisture from my mouth. It was going to happen. There was no way out.

"Mmm ... mmm ... mmm ... my innn ... innn... inhaler." I wanted to crawl under the table. I was thankful no one besides her could hear me, but that was bad enough. I couldn't look at her.

"Anything else" she asked, as if she didn't even hear me stuttering. She didn't laugh at me at all. No one had ever passed up a chance to laugh at me before.

I showed her my Epi-pen and told her about my allergies. She didn't even laugh at my flashlight and whistle. "I'm afraid of the dark, too," she said. I showed her my bug collection container, tweezers, and magnifying glass. "In case I ever find an injured insect that needs help," I told her. I wanted to show her the letter my dad had written to me before he got on the airplane ... and the four quarters I had been carrying in my survival pack since the day he left. Those were my favorite things in the world. *Maybe later. Maybe if we become good friends, I'll show her then.*

"Class, let's get started," the teacher said. "There's a manila folder on your table. You'll need to take it home and have your parents sign the papers in them." Her voice was nicer than Mrs. Blueberry's. She smiled when she talked, and there were no wrinkles on her forehead.

"I'm Mrs. Wallazendedias," she paused to give the class a chance to laugh at her name, which I'm guessing she had gotten use to. They did. So did I. Her name sounded a lot funnier than Mrs. Blueberry's. Way funnier. Mrs. Wallazendedias never broke her smile. Once the class calmed down a bit, she continued. "It is funny, isn't it?" She laughed, too, for a minute. "You are more than welcome to call me Mrs. W. or Mrs. Walla, if it's easier. Either one is fine with me."

She walked around the room, introducing each student as she came to them. Only twenty-four students in this class. Six tables on each side of the room. Twelve sets of partners. Boys and girls were split right down the middle, twelve and twelve. *I wonder if they planned it that way.* I saw a couple of kids from this morning's math class. Out of all of them, there were only three faces I had ever seen before.

"We're going to have a lot of fun, " she said. "We have several field trips planned, which is why I need those papers signed, and we will also have a few projects."

Everyone groaned. *Projects, yuck.* Science was my favorite subject, but in no way did I want to do any projects.

"The good news is you'll be doing them with your partner. The bad news is ... I hope you like your partner." She laughed so hard it sounded like it came from her toes and worked its way up to her belly. That made the rest of us laugh.

I definitely like my partner.

"Also in your folder is a list of assignments you'll need to complete this year." Mrs. Walla waited for us to sift through our folder. "I know," she said, "it seems like a lot. Most of them are small projects that should only take you an hour or two to put together." She made another trip around the room and stopped at the table with two dark-haired boys who could have been twins. Maybe they were.

"Remember, class. The big one is due at the end of May, just before school lets out." The taller of the two boys, Jamie Gomiller, blew out a long sigh of relief. So did a few other people.

"Don't let the next few months fool you. Yes, you have plenty of time, but it's going to take a lot of preparation for this project in order to make a good grade. And this project alone counts for half of your grade."

"Half," Kevin Stalling complained. He threw his hands in the air and then smacked them against the table. "That isn't fair" he shouted. His face turned bright red and a vein in his neck popped out.

"Yes, Mr. Stalling. Half. I suggest you get busy," Mrs. Walla said. She walked right over to his table and stood in front of him. But, instead of getting mad like Mrs. Blueberry, she smiled and leaned in to whisper. She spoke so softly, in fact, that it is was difficult to hear her. "And one more thing, Mr. Stalling," she stopped for a minute and looked at the rest of us. "The rest of you should know this, too. Fair is irrelevant. Life isn't fair at all. Learn that now. You can't sit around waiting for life to be fair in order to be happy."

No one spoke. The room was so silent I could hear Kevin breathing from across the room.

"Well, that's my tidbit of friendly advice for the day. Take it and do with it what you will. As far as the assignments, start thinking about what you want to do for your project. Work together with your partner to come up with an idea you both feel comfortable with. And that means you will need to exchange phone numbers. Do it today."

Exchange phone numbers? Elizabeth Faith-Grace Winkworth will have to give me her phone number? We are going to have to talk on the phone and work together for the next six months? Awesome.

The bell rang. The windows rattled. The bell was so loud everyone covered their ears. I don't remember the bells from my last school being so loud, but I guess the older a person gets, the louder the bell needs to be ... and I *am* almost twelve years old.

Before I could get the nerve to say anything, Elizabeth had crammed her manila folder into her backpack and run out the door without giving me her number. I got my things together as fast as I could and tried running after her. By the time I made it to the hallway, there were about a million kids. *Ugh!*

The rest of the day was a blur. Two more classes. Almost sixty more classmates. Most were unfamiliar faces. Some weren't ... and some I hoped to never see again.

~ *4* ~

Mmmm. Bacon! My most favorite smell in the world. And two days in a row! I ran down the hall, still in my pajamas, and there it was. The biggest plate of bacon I had ever seen.

"Think you can eat some today," Mom asked. "I even got your plate down for you."

"Awww, Mommy had to get your plate for you." Jared was waiting on the couch. *Does he ever sleep*? It sure didn't seem like it if he did. No matter how early I got up, he was up waiting to pick a fight or make fun of me.

"You're not that much bigger than me, you know." I should have known better. I did know better. Before I could stop myself or change the subject, Jared jumped from the couch and was taunting me to stand back-to-back with him.

"Come on. Let's see," he demanded. He stood there with his hand right at the top of his head, daring me to find out exactly how much taller he really was. If only there was somewhere to hide. Anywhere. There wasn't. I would have to take my punishment like a man.

So I did. I turned my back to him. I took four big steps until our backs touched. *I bet my skin is going to melt off from touching the evil minion.*

"Mom," Jared yelled. "Come hold your hands above our heads at the same time so we can see." He bounced up and down, waiting for Mom to agree. She didn't want to. I could tell. Her shoulder dropped way down and the smile she had just a few minutes ago was gone.

"Jared, you know you're taller than Philip. Why must you do this?" She wiped her hands on her apron and stood next to us.

"He started it," Jared said.

"But you're two years older than your brother. Shouldn't you be acting just a little more mature by now?" The muscles in her jaw moved up and down while she stared right into his eyes. They were nose-to-nose. Yeah, she was mad. I loved it when she got mad at him for being mean to me.

"Okay, you can look now."

"See that, Philly-Willy?" He stuck his tongue out and pointed to Mom's hands. "I've got you by nearly a foot."

"Who cares? I'll be taller than you one day and when I am..." I balled my fist, showing him what he had to look forward to.

"Alright, you two, breakfast. I've got a doctor's appointment, so I'll need to leave before you." She put one hand on her hip and pointed a finger from the other hand, back and forth between Jared and me. "You had better be ready to leave before I go." She smacked her hands together. "Get moving."

Doctor's appointment? She hadn't mentioned a doctor's appointment before now. She never ever went to the doctor, unless something was really bad wrong, and nothing had ever been really bad wrong.

Jared must have been thinking the same thing because he followed me to my room and wasn't even being mean to me for once.

"Did you know anything about Mom going to the doctor" he asked. He sat down on my bed and threw his legs up, crossing one over the over. He leaned way back against the head of my bed and put his hands behind his neck. "She hasn't said anything to me. What about you" he asked again.

I couldn't even speak. I shook my head. I sat down next to him and, for a few minutes, neither of us said a word. Not even to argue.

"I wish Dad was here," I confessed. "He would know what to do. He always knows what to do." We were quiet for a few more minutes before Jared went right back to being the mean big brother he had always been.

"Yeah, well, I bet she tells me what's going on before she tells you." Jared smacked his hand against my head and ran out of my room, laughing.

Dear Jesus, it's me ... Philippian Macedon from 222 Carthage Road. Two days in a row! Must be a record-breaker, huh? I don't know if You know it or not, but my mom is going to the doctor today and I have no idea why. Please, Jesus, don't let my mom die. Please. Amen.

For the rest of the week, I felt like I was walking through a deep foggy forest, trying to find the way out. Mom still hadn't told us why she had gone to the doctor, and I had been too afraid to ask. I guess Jared had, too, because he hadn't said a word about it yet.

"Are you okay, Philippian?" Elizabeth had spoken very little during the week, and I still didn't have her number. I really didn't care too much either, since there were other things to worry about. More important things.

"Yeah, I ... I ... I'm okay. Just got some st ... st ... stuff on my mmm .... mmm ... mmm ... mind."

She never seemed to mind my stuttering and, for that, I was very thankful. Especially on days like today.

"Mmm ... mmm .... mmm ... mind." The two girls at the table next to us were pointing at me and mocking me. I'm sure my cheeks were flushed, because I suddenly got very hot, and sweat was coming from the top of my head.

"Stop it!" Elizabeth stood and yelled at them to stop picking on me.

"Elizabeth and Philippian sitting in a tree," the girls sang loud enough half the class joined in. "K. I. S. S. I. N. G. First comes love. Then comes mmm ... mmm ... mmm ... marriage."

I ran as fast as I could from class. I left so fast I left all my stuff on the desk. I kept running. And running. I ran all the way around to the back of the school, behind the gym. I ran until I found a foot trail behind the school.

Why me, Jesus? Why? Why did I get cursed with this stuttering? It isn't fair! I couldn't even pray out loud. Or maybe I just didn't want to.

"Fair is irrelevant. Life isn't fair at all. Learn that now. You can't sit around waiting for life to be fair in order to be happy." I could hear Mrs. Walla's words, just like the day she said them. She was right. Life isn't fair. It isn't fair that I stutter when I'm nervous. It isn't fair that I'm shorter than everyone in the whole school. It isn't fair my mom is sick, and there is nothing I could do about it.

Life isn't fair at all!

Angst of the Middle-school Newbie

~ 5 ~

We had just gotten up from dinner when the doorbell rang. Jared ran to the door, sure it was one of his friends. It usually was.

"Philly-Willy! There's a *girl* here to see *you*!"

I was almost afraid to go to the door. No, I was *very* afraid. *It's probably one of those girls from science class.*

"Philly-Willy" Jared yelled louder.

"Okay, okay, already." I ran to the kitchen and tried peeking out the window, but I couldn't reach it. *Of course.* There was nothing left to do but face the music. I pushed my glasses back up my nose and walked to the door.

"Philippian." Her voice sounded like an angel's. I was sure that's how angels must sound when they speak. *She* was an angel. "I got your address from Eric Holden." Elizabeth pointed at the house with green shutters down the road.

I shrugged.

"We're in English together, and he said he knows your brother. I hope you don't mind."

Mind? Are you crazy? Of course I don't mind.

"Www ... www... why are you hhh ... hhh ... here?"

"Well, we have a science project to work on and you still haven't asked for my phone number." She handed me a piece of paper. "Now you have it."

"Th ... Th ..."

"Really, Philippian?" Elizabeth put both hands on her hips and stared at me. "I've heard you talk to other kids in our science class. You don't stutter when you talk to them. You need to get over it and talk to me without being nervous." She grabbed my hand and yanked me through the door. "Let's walk."

"Mom, I'll be back" I yelled, and closed the door behind me.

"See! And another thing, you can call me 'Izzy'. That's what my friends call me."

Friends? Am I her friend now?

We walked for a while without talking. We walked side by side all the way around the neighborhood, and then it hit me ... *even she is taller than me. Why?*

Please, Jesus, I prayed while we walked. *It's me, Philippian Macedon from 222 Carthage Road. Could You please help me? Help me talk to Izzy Winkworth from science class without stuttering. Just once. Please, Jesus. Amen.*

"What's your bracelet say?" Izzy pointed to the red bracelet I have been wearing every single day since my seventh birthday. My dad gave it to me. "You should always remember what your name means," he said to me every day until he left on the plane.

I turned my wrist so she could read it herself without me having to talk, but she wouldn't allow it.

"Nope. I want to hear you read it ... without stuttering." She stopped in front of me so I couldn't walk anymore. "There is no reason to be nervous around me, Philippian Macedon." She crossed her arms and tapped her foot on the ground. "Now, read it."

Please, Jesus. Here goes.

"Um, it says, 'Philippians four-thirteen'." *So far so good.* "For I can do all things through Christ who strengthens me!" I did it! I did it!

Izzy clapped her hands and high-fived me. "See? I knew it." And then the most wonderful thing ever happened! Izzy hugged *me*! Me! I thought I would choke from excitement. I felt my heart in my throat and I couldn't swallow at all.

"Is that the reason your parents named you Philippian? Because of that verse?"

It took me a few seconds to speak again. Once I was finally able to, I said. "I was born on April thirteenth. Philippians four-thirteen. Tah-da!"

"How cool." We were on our second time around the neighborhood when I had the best idea ever. The best.

"Hey, do you like nature trails?"

Izzy nodded. Her black pony tail bounced all around. I grabbed her hand just like she had done mine earlier. We ran past my house without my mom or Jared noticing, and ran between the next two neighbors' houses. Behind all of the two-story houses on Carthage Road was the best nature trail I had ever been on. It was my secret. And now it was going to be *our* secret.

The trail narrowed as we walked. It was so narrow, in fact, Izzy and I had to walk in single file. She followed behind me, holding on to the strap of my camouflage survival pack. We walked until we came to a big tree that had fallen.

"Can we rest here" she asked. She sat down before I could answer. It was my favorite spot. The place I ran to when Jared was being mean; when none of the other kids on Carthage Road wanted to ride bikes with me. When I worried about my mom or missed my dad. This was *my* spot.

"Shhh!" I held my finger over my mouth. "Listen". My ears perked and my skin tingled. I heard the click ... click ... clicking. Izzy scrunched her eyebrows. I gave her a minute to hear it. After all, she wasn't use to the woods like me. "Listen real close. You hear that clicking?" *Wow, my stuttering went away really fast*, I thought while I was waiting for Izzy to hear what I heard. I was surprised, but I *did* pray, so I guess it made sense.

"What am I listening for?" She cupped her hand behind her ear to hear better. I'm not sure if it helped but after a few seconds she nodded. "Oh."

"That's an insect. An injured insect." I unzipped the front pouch of my survival kit and pulled out my insect collection container, tweezers, and magnifying glass. Even with my coke-bottle glasses, as Jared always called them, I needed the magnifying glass to find the insect. It could have been anywhere but, by the sound of the clicking, I could tell it was close.

"How can you tell it's injured" Izzy whispered. She followed me as I tiptoed around the log, searching for the insect.

"That's the sound they make when they are injured. Then the ants come protect them from other bigger insects that might eat them."

"The ants don't eat them" she asked, her voice raising to a much higher pitch.

"Shh." I found it. Right there on a seedling was an orange butterfly with black dots in the center and black tipped wings. It was beautiful. But one of its wings had been torn, and it was no longer able to fly.

"It's okay, little one." I opened my collection container. I lifted the butterfly with my tweezers and lowered it into the container. The lid had four holes drilled in the top for air. When I closed it, the butterfly was still able to breathe.

"If I don't take care of him, he will die. This is my job." I let Izzy hold the butterfly.

"Can you tell if it's a boy or girl" she asked. I had never had someone interested in my insects before. Mostly Jared and his buddies picked on me, calling me "bug eyes" or "bug guy".

"I can, but I won't be able to until I get it home and can examine it a little better." I tucked the container back in my survival pack and zipped it only halfway. "Wanna see something else?" I waited for her answer. I couldn't believe I was actually going to share my two favorite things in the world with Izzy. I hadn't even shared them with my mom yet.

Izzy nodded and I unzipped another pocket in my survival pack. I pulled out the letter from my dad and four quarters. Before she could ask, I explained.

"My dad left twelve days ago. He went to Iraq." My eyes started burning a little so I stopped long enough to take a long, deep breath. Then I continued. "He's my best friend. My *only* friend. The night before he left, he wrote me this letter. He told me anytime I'm having a hard time with anything, to go to my favorite spot and read this."

Izzy held out her hand. "Can *I* read it?" I handed it over. She was careful when opening it. It was a bit worn after being opened and refolded so many times, but she was careful, and I liked that about her.

Dear Philippian,

I know you don't feel it right now, but you are a very strong and brave boy. People may pick on you because of your size, you may think you're weak, but I have news for you. You can do all things through Christ who strengthens you. All things. Not some. All. That, my son, is the very reason you are named Philippian. We prayed for nine months about what to name you. Then you were born on the thirteenth of April, and it couldn't have been any clearer. That was to be your name.

Son, I was small like you when I was a kid. Everyone picked on me. I felt like I had no one to turn to. I had no father. No older brother. It was just me and my mom, and she was too lonely to notice how sad I was. I'm not small anymore. And some day, you won't be either. But know that nothing will ever happen that God won't be right there to see you through. That is what you have to hold onto. You can do all things through Christ. All things.

Take care of your mom for me until I get home. I love you all the way around the world two times and back again.

Always, Dad.

Izzy carefully folded the letter, following all the same folds. She handed it to me and shook her head. "Wow," she said. "You must really miss your dad."

"I do."

"What about the quarters? What are they for?"

I held them tight in my hand. I loved to hold them in my hands when I had something bad on my mind or when I had a problem I needed to solve. I held my hand open and let her take them. No one else had ever held them before. No one but me and Dad.

"My dad said the day I was born he went to the drink machine while he waiting for my mom to deliver me. He put in a dollar bill. When the drink came out, so did these four quarters... all with the year I was born written on them. He said he knew then it would be the luckiest day of his life. He kept the quarters ever since, and when he left for Iraq, he gave them to me to hold until he gets back."

Izzy gave them back to me and smiled. "You were wrong about something, Philippian Macedon."

"Huh" I asked.

Izzy put her hand on top of mine and squeezed my fingers. "You were wrong. Your dad is *not* your only friend. I am your friend, too, Philippian."

Angst of the Middle-school Newbie

We must have been gone a little too long because Mom called the police when she couldn't find me. My mom isn't really a worry-wart but, for some reason, she was worried something bad had happened to me.

Izzy's parents were worried, too. They went to my house looking for her and when no one could find us, three police cars came over to ask questions. They asked for recent pictures and what we were wearing. They knocked on every door in the neighborhood, thinking I might have gone to one of the other kids' houses. They had no idea I had no friends ... at least I didn't until I met Izzy.

Izzy hadn't lived in her house long enough to make friends, and I just never did. The only thing the neighborhood kids knew about me was that I was short, wore funny-looking glasses, and rode an ugly girl's bike. They didn't know my birthday or that I rescued injured insects. They didn't know how much I missed my dad, or that I wanted to be an entomologist when I grow up. They knew nothing at all about me.

They searched my room for any idea of where I might have gone. They blocked off roads. They were getting ready to bring out hunting dogs when we made our way from the trail. There was barely enough light left in the day to make our way out. I wasn't worried about getting lost, though. I had walked this trail a million times since we first moved in six years ago. I could have found my way out blindfolded.

"I wonder what's going on." Izzy stayed close beside me, as if I could actually protect her from something. As if I was her hero.

I saw all the police cars and my heart almost dropped to my toes. *Mom*! I started running straight to my house, afraid something had happened to her. Afraid God had taken her while I was on the trail.

Izzy ran fast behind me, keeping up with my every step. My cheeks burned. I fought for every breath. I kept running anyway.

"Please, Jesus," I prayed out loud. I didn't have time to tell Him who I was or give Him my address. I could only hope by now He knew. "Please let my mom be okay. Please, Jesus. Let her be okay."

I ran as fast as I could, Izzy tagging behind. As soon as I got to my front door, my strong running legs melted to warm jello. I fell to the floor, two feet inside the door. I dug for my inhaler in my survival pack. I couldn't find it. Everything around me faded into a large black hole.

"Here, Philippian. Take this. Breathe, Philippian!" Izzy shook my inhaler and shoved it in my mouth, pushing the medicine into the chamber. She was *my* hero. Finally, a deep breath!

"Young lady, where have you been?" Izzy's father crinkled his forehead. "We've been looking for you for hours!" His loud voice rumbled. I felt it with my next good breath.

"You were supposed to be studying!" He continued to yell. "You were supposed to be home two-and-a-half hours ago." His finger shook when he pointed it in her face. I wanted to yell at him the way he was yelling at her. I wanted to stand up for her, to tell him it was my fault. And it was. But, before I could do anything, Mom was yelling at *me*.

"Do you have any idea what I have been thinking for the past two hours?" Her swollen eyes proved she had been crying.

Jared walked up and punched me right in the arm. "Way to go, punk!" He blew on his knuckles and waved his fist at me. "Don't let it happen again. You had Mom worried to death."

"Where were you" Mom asked. "I thought you were dead. I thought someone took you. I thought... " She stopped. She covered her face with her hands and the tears streamed down her cheeks all over again.

"I'm sorry, Mom. I just went for a walk. I just…" There was nothing else to say. No amount of talking would make things better tonight. I was more worried about Izzy being in trouble. I was worried she wouldn't want to be my friend anymore.

"Let's go!" Her dad pulled her by her arm and speed walked to their car. She looked back at me, but said nothing. Not a word.

It took several hours, but things finally calmed down at our house. The police left, the neighbors returned to their homes, and Mom finally stopped crying. I had never seen her so upset, and knowing it was my fault made me feel horrible. I know my dad would understand, but he wasn't here to help.

I hugged Mom and apologized for the seventeen-hundredth time. Not that it helped much. When I went to my room, I heard her crying again.

Dear Jesus, it's me, Philippian Macedon from 222 Carthage Road. You know, the kid who screwed everything up today. First, I should probably tell You I'm sorry. I hope I didn't let You down like I did my mom. And thank You for not letting her die today. It scared me when I saw all the police cars. Jesus, I really like Izzy Winkworth. I wish Dad was here so I could tell him about it. So can I just tell You? She's the only person who has ever been nice to me. I hope she's nice to me tomorrow, seeing how I got her in trouble and all. Anyway, if You talk to my dad, could You tell him I miss him? Tell him I love him all the way around the world two times and back again. Thank You. Amen.

As soon as I got off my knees, I remembered. "The butterfly!" I had forgotten all about the poor little thing. "You're going to need something to eat ... and a name."

I lifted the butterfly, spreading its wings to take a better look. I promised Izzy I would. I always keep my promises. "Yep, you're a girl. Just like I thought. How would you like to be called Faith-Grace? Yeah, that looks good on you. Faith-Grace."

I searched the kitchen and I found a jar in the lower cabinet. I hammered three big holes in the lid. There was a half-eaten apple on the counter Jared must have left out. "Perfect. I'll make you a more suitable home this weekend. This will do for now." Faith-Grace would sleep comfortably on my bedside table tonight. I left her there and went to check on Mom one more time before going to bed.

"Mom," I knocked on her bedroom door.

"Come in, Sweetie." She didn't sound mad any more. She sat on the side of the bed, holding a picture of Dad. She smiled any time she looked at him.

"I miss him so much," she said. I sat next to her, and she put her arm around me like nothing had happened.

"Me too."

We sat for a few minutes without saying a word. It was nice to just be quiet together. It was nice for just a few minutes to not have Jared laughing at me or punching me. I secretly wished it could be this way all the time.

"When's Dad coming home?" I hadn't asked that question before tonight. I guess I have always been afraid of the answer. Anytime I missed him, I just read my letter. Any other time he had been deployed, he was able to email or call home. This time he isn't allowed to and that makes it harder on all of us. Especially me and Mom.

"It'll be a while. I know it feels like he's been gone forever, but it's really only been a little while." She ran her fingers through my hair and brushed it away from my glasses. "You know, he's usually gone a year."

We both took a deep breath and thought about it for a few seconds. Almost eleven months. Eleven long months, without hearing from him.

"I'm sorry again that I scared you tonight. I didn't mean to."

She wrapped both arms around me and squeezed tighter than she ever had before. "I know, Sweetie. I know. I'm just glad you're okay." She kissed the top of my head. "You remind me so much of your father in so many ways."

"Good ways" I asked.

"There is no other way," she answered.

"Mom," I had to ask. I had been wanting to for weeks now. "Why did you have to go to the doctor the other day?" I didn't want to say it. I didn't want to hear those words coming from my own lips but I had to. "Are you dying?"

Mom laughed. First only a giggle but then it turned into a full belly laugh. I laughed with her, even though I didn't know why we were laughing.

"No, I'm not dying, you crazy kid!" She kissed my forehead and she wasn't even checking my temperature.

"You promise you're not dying? You never go to the doctor."

She stopped laughing and put her hands on my cheeks. She looked right at me and, with the most serious face I had ever seen my mom make, she said, "I'm not dying. I'm having a baby."

~ 7 ~

I couldn't wait to get to school. I wasn't really too excited about school. It was science class I couldn't wait for. Really, it was Izzy. I had so much to tell her. The butterfly is a girl and I named her Faith-Grace. My mom is having a baby. I wasn't quite sure how I felt about that yet. I already had one sibling I didn't like. What if I didn't like the new one? What if it didn't like me? What if this one was Dad's favorite and he stopped hanging out with me when he was home?

So many questions and no one to run by them. No one but Izzy. I still didn't know if she was mad at me about Friday night. It had been a very long weekend not knowing. She hadn't come by like I hoped she would and I didn't dare call. I was too afraid her dad would answer. Afraid he would still be mad.

Since I wasn't able to talk to her all weekend, I wrote her a note. Science class could not come soon enough. I would give her the note and, if after reading it, she was smiling, I would know everything was okay and we were still friends. If not ... well, that just wasn't an option yet. *She has to still be my friend. I don't have any other friends.*

The bell rang and I ran as fast as I could to get to class. I wanted to see her more than anything.

"Excuse you," Brandon Nealy said when he almost knocked me down coming through the door. *Excuse me?* I wanted to point out his mistake. But he was two good feet taller and probably fifty pounds heavier. I didn't stand a chance. He could clobber me with one punch and probably would if I said anything.

So I said nothing. I lowered my head and walked to my table. I rehearsed what I would say while I waited for Izzy. I was going to apologize, offer to call her dad and apologize to him, too. I really didn't want to do that, but if that's what it took to keep her as my friend, I would just suck it up and take my licks like a man.

I watched the clock. It was almost five minutes after. If Izzy didn't get to class soon, she would be late, and then she would have after-school detention. I wanted to throw up waiting for her to get there. *Might as well reread my letter while I wait.* I looked through the side pockets of my backpack. I was sure that's where I had put it. I could be wrong. I looked through the large inside pocket. Then the back pocket. I searched my survival pack. I stood and searched my jean pockets. Then I searched them all again.

Nothing!

As the bell began to ring, Izzy ran through the door, out of breath. Mrs. Walla smiled and welcomed her to class, showing no signs of anger. Much better than Miss Blueberry. Miss Blueberry would have blasted her in front of the entire class.

Izzy sat beside me and took out her books without looking up or speaking. I wanted to tell her how sorry I was, but it was time for class and Mrs. Walla was going over the assignments for the week. I wasn't listening to anything she was saying until she called on the girls in the table next to us. The mean ones. The bullies. That drew my attention.

"What's so funny, ladies" she asked, walking towards them with her hand out. "Care to share with the class?"

Amanda, the louder and meaner of the two laughed, and handed her a note. "Sure, go ahead." She looked right at me and laughed. That's when I knew. She had my letter. The letter I had spent hours writing to Izzy. My private letter.

Mrs. Walla walked back to the front of the class and unfolded the letter. She cleared her throat the way only an adult could do right before handing down a punishment, and began to read ... out loud ... to the whole class.

"Dear Elizabeth Faith-Grace Winkworth," she began. There was nowhere to hide. No way to warn Izzy of the things I had said in my most vulnerable moments over the weekend. Nothing I could do to stop the inevitable. All I could do was cover my face with my hands and pray it ended quickly.

I wish you would call. I wish you would come over and let me know you are okay. That you aren't mad at me. That you are still my friend. You are my only friend, besides my dad, and he's going to be gone for a really long time. So, for now, that makes you the only friend I have and right now. I miss you so much.

The entire class laughed. I heard the whispers. I heard my name floating through the room. *Please, Jesus. Please make her stop.* I wanted to run out of the room but I knew Mrs. Walla wouldn't allow it.

She stopped reading to correct the class and bring order. "Tell me, Amanda, how did you come to have this letter since it is neither addressed to you or by you? That would means it is not your property." She folded her arms in front of her and waited for an explanation.

Amanda wasn't embarrassed at all. Her face wasn't red like Izzy's. She didn't want to hide like me. She cocked her head back. She was proud of herself. She laughed and pointed, "He dropped it at the door."

Even better. Now everyone knows I wrote the letter. As if it wasn't bad enough already, Izzy was sure to be mad at me forever.

"So Philippian dropped his property and, instead of doing the right thing and giving it back to him, you thought you would keep it and then use it to embarrass him? Is that about right?" Mrs. Walla folded the letter back up and walked to my desk, still staring at Amanda. She slid the letter to me and patted me on the back. I wanted to die, to melt away to nothing like the Wicked Witch of the West. I wanted to disappear into thin air and never return.

"Actually, Mrs. W," she said, pointing to her lab partner, "Sarah picked it up and gave it to me. So it's her fault."

Sarah huffed.

Finally the two of them were going to get what they deserved. They were the meanest girls in class and they never got in trouble for it.

"So, your friend did something wrong and you joined her. Did your mother ever ask you if you would jump too if your friend jumped off a bridge?"

The two mean girls had nothing else to say. For the first time since the first day of school, they were silent and embarrassed. If I wasn't still mortified from my own humiliation, I would have loved to watch this show.

"How about you two meet me after school this afternoon? And let your parents know you'll be meeting me every afternoon for two weeks."

I wanted to cheer, to stand and applaud Mrs. Walla for finally doing something about them. I wanted to laugh in their faces. But I couldn't. Izzy wouldn't even look at me and I knew this meant I had lost my new friend. I was right back to where I started. No friends, and the butt of everyone's jokes.

Angst of the Middle-school Newbie

~ *8* ~

When I woke this morning, I wanted to pray. I wanted to ask Jesus to fix the mess I caused with Izzy. To make her my friend again. To please make people stop picking on me. I wanted to ask Jesus to please bring my dad home real soon. I had so many things I wanted to ask Jesus, but when I got on my knees beside my bed and folded my hands, nothing happened. I couldn't bring myself to speak at all. I was stuck.

Mom says Jesus can hear me praying even if I can't speak. I don't know how He could hear me if I haven't said anything, but Mom promised He could. Hopefully she is right because, if not, I haven't talked to Jesus in a long time.

I wonder if it's true. If Jesus knows and loves even me. Dad said that Jesus knew me before I was even born. That He knew everything about me and loved me even then. There are so many people in the world. So many other kids. I wonder how He knows us all and, even if He does, how He has time to listen to all of our prayers. I guess it might be a good thing that I have taken a few days off. I bet He needed a break.

Many days had passed since Izzy went on the trails with me. It felt like even longer since she stopped talking to me. I miss my friend.

The school halls are still crowded, but no one speaks to me. Not one person. Well, that's not entirely true. Jared speaks to me every time he sees me in the hallway. So do his friends.

"Philly-Willy. How's life down there?"

"Hey Coke-Bottles, how are things looking?"

"Hey twerp, whatcha got in that fanny pack?"

"Want any peanuts?"

They always had something to say. Nothing nice. I was used to that. They laughed at my hair, calling me "Shaggy Dog" and "Mop Head".

"When are you going to fix that mop?"

"You need to take that mutt to get groomed."

Other than that, nothing. Wednesdays were the worst. Dodge ball in P.E. It was the only day I wasn't invisible, though I wanted to be. On Wednesday, everyone knew my name, though few used it and it had become the common goal to knock my glasses off my face.

I hated Wednesdays.

I wonder what next year will be like, when I am not in the "new-kid" group of sixth graders. When I am a seventh grader and a little further up the totem pole. I wonder if I'll make any friends. Maybe I'll be able to give them some of my wisdom on how to avoid the big kids, and how to keep from being stuffed in a locker or shoved into the girl's bathroom. Those would be valuable lessons to have as a new kid. Yeah, that's what I'll do. I'll start writing down all my thoughts of wisdom and pass them along at the beginning of next year to any "wanderers".

"Mr. Macedon, you care to join us," Mrs. Walla asked, interrupting my deep thoughts. I had no idea how long I had been daydreaming but, judging by the way she was tapping her fingers over her folded arms, and her squinted eyes, it must have been quite some time.

"Um ... yeah .. uh.." I had no idea what she had even been talking about, so I had nothing to add. My knees knocked so hard against each other, I'm sure everyone in the entire class heard them.

"Do I need to call your mother, Mr. Macedon? You've been daydreaming a lot lately, and you haven't turned in a single assignment in two weeks." I had never seen her angry. She was my fun teacher. My laid-back-anything-goes teacher. Science was my best subject and this was my "pie-class". Or at least I thought it would be.

I raised my shoulders. Apparently that was not the right thing to do because, the next thing I knew, I am staying after school joining the detention chain gang.

I don't remember the rest of the day. I watched the clock, waiting for the hour that I would take my walk of shame; the long, dreaded walk down the sixth grade hallway to report for my punishment. I even had to wait in line to report for duty.

A small voice from behind broke the boredom of waiting. "What are you in for?" I almost didn't hear him. I heard a noise but had no idea this kid was speaking to me. He asked again, "Why are you in detention?"

"Me," I asked, pointing to myself. I pushed the hair from my face that had fallen in front of my glasses. I hadn't seen him before. Not even in the lunchroom or hallways. Not on the playground or at the bicycle rack.

I must have been staring at him or something, because he snapped his fingers in front of my face. "Hey, you awake in there," he asked.

"Um ... sorry," I finally forced myself to speak. "I uh ... I was daydreaming in class. So ..." I wasn't sure if I was imagining things or if Jesus had actually heard some of my prayers and this was my answer.

"Daydreaming," he asked, sounding shocked. "That's your crime?" He chuckled and shook his head. "Well, I was caught talking in class instead of paying attention." He seemed proud of his offense.

"Not my first time, so I guess this will teach me to keep my mouth shut."

He shook his head, tossing his hair from one side to the other. His hair wasn't nearly as long as mine, but it was definitely longer than that of the other boys in most of my classes.

"My name is Michael Donavon Schmitzer, but you can just call me Mike or Michael," the blond-haired kid said. "What's yours?" He held out his hand and waited for me to take it. Izzy was the only other kid in my whole life who had shaken my hand. It took me a second, but I finally took his hand and gave it a squeeze.

"Philippian Macedon." My eyes were still as large as Wednesday afternoon dodge-balls. I can't say with one-hundred-percent certainty, but I am pretty sure my mouth was hanging wide open the whole time.

"Mind if I call you 'Phil'? Your name is a mouthful." He laughed. Not at me. He just laughed, as if he didn't have a care in the world. As if he had a million friends and no one had ever picked on him. Ever.

But how could that be, I wondered. How could a kid like Michael Donavon Schmitzer have gotten through this cruel world unscathed?

"What's wrong? Cat got your tongue?" He laughed again, slapping his hand against his leg as if he had just heard the funniest joke ever.

I straightened up and looked him square in the eye. This was no laughing matter. "No, I'm good. So, how long did they give you" I asked Michael.

"Just today. Mrs. Manta said if I came to class tomorrow with my act together, my time would be served." He shoved his hands in his front pockets. "Not sure I can do it, though. My dad says I am just a born talker. Can't help myself."

I sized him up, starting from his loosely-laced high-tops all the way up to his care-free dirty-blond hair. He was an interesting-looking kid. No glasses or anything like that, but still interesting. He seemed ... happy. Oddly enough. As if nothing stuck to him.

"What's up" he asked with both his eyebrows crossed. "Why are you looking at me like that?" He seemed genuinely curious. Not angry, but curious.

"Well," I said. I shook my head. "It's just that, well, I have never met anyone in my whole life who's ... who's actually shorter than *me*."

~ *9* ~

Turns out, Michael and I had a lot more in common than being the short kids on the block. We both had mean older brothers who loved to pick on us. He was the middle kid, and I would soon be the middle kid. He loved insects and reptiles even. He had been picked on his whole life by older, bigger kids ... just like me.

The difference in the two of us, though, was that Michael never seemed to be bothered by it. He was always smiling and laughing. Even when the big kids picked on him, he was nice to them. He seemed genuinely unfazed by their cruelty, and I was amazed, to say the least.

"Want to come to my house tonight? Since it's a weekend, I can have company." Michael invited *me* to his house. Me! No one had ever invited me to their house before. "I've got a python you'll want to see." His eyes got huge as he stretched his arms as wide as he could. "That thing's this big. You've got to see it!"

"Sure, and I'll bring Faith-Grace! You'll like her. She's beautiful."

"Faith-Grace?"

"Oh, yeah, I forgot I haven't told you. She's my butterfly. I found her a while back with a broken wing. I built her a terrarium so she has a safe place to live since she can't stay in the woods on her own anymore."

"Great. See you tonight."

We parted in the hallway to go to our second-period classes. We had no classes together but managed to pass in the hallway between each class. I had never had a friend in the hallway before. Other than, I had never had a friend at all. I wanted so badly to tell her about him. I bet she would be happy for me.

I looked up just in time to see her as she walked through the door. Other than talking to Michael in the hallway, this was my favorite part of the day. Her long black hair bounced every time one of her feet touched the floor. She wore her backpack, using only one shoulder strap. *Brave*, I thought. Sometimes she smiled, just not at me. Her eyes were focused and her cheeks were never puffed up like they would be if she laughed or smiled a lot. To me, she looked like she was either in deep thought ... or sad. I hadn't decided which yet. *I hope she isn't sad.*

Izzy took her seat next to me, as she had done every single day since school started. She tossed her black and pink camouflage backpack on the floor and dug out her science book, pencil, and journal. She organized her supplies on the table in perfect order, as always: her book on the left, journal on the right, and her pencil at the top of the desk, just beyond the two. It was the same way every day. But, today, for some reason, something seemed different. I hadn't quite put my finger on it yet, but I knew something was different.

"Are you okay" I leaned over and whispered before Mrs. Walla started handing out our Friday quiz.

"Yeah. I'll talk to you about it later," she whispered without looking up to catch me staring at her.

She'll talk to me about it later? Did I hear her right? Is that what she said? She hadn't spoken to me in weeks. Not a single word. My mind raced. My heart matched its pace. Was she actually going to talk to me again? I could hardly sit still to hold a thought in my head. *And when is later? Like after class? After school? Or next week, later? Which one?* I needed more details. More information. I needed to ask more questions, but I was too afraid to push my luck. I had to know! I rubbed my hands across my thighs, trying to get rid of the sweat on my palms. By the time I managed to build up enough courage to ask just one more question, Mrs. Walla was walking around the room, handing out the quiz. My questions would have to wait.

Mrs. Walla looked down her nose at me as she handed me the quiz. "You're going to do well, right, Mr. Macedon" she asked in her best mothering voice. I just nodded. I had no answer. A nod would have to do. She walked away, and immediately I started worrying.

How would I make it through this quiz when Izzy would be talking to me later? How could I possibly think of anything else?

"Alright, class," Mrs. Walla called for everyone's attention. Once everyone had made eye contact, she continued, "You have thirty minutes to take this quiz. Afterward, I want you to work with your partners on your science project. Do so quietly, please. I'll have your grades available before the end of class." She turned to check the time on the clock. She pointed and said, "Thirty minutes. So, at eleven-o-five, pencils must be down and quizzes turned in. Ready? You may start ... now."

I looked down at the questions in front of me. I tried to focus. I pushed my glasses higher up on my nose, hoping that would help. It didn't. The words were still blurry. Maybe it was more my mind than the questions. Either way, I had no idea what was on that quiz.

I looked around the room. Everyone was scribbling away. No one else looked up, so I must have been the only person lost.

Get it together, Philippian. You have to pass this test. Failing was not an option. Failing would mean restriction. It would mean I couldn't go to Michael's house. It would mean no trail hikes or time alone at my favorite spot. Extra chores. Harassment from my perfect older brother. Disappointment from my mom or worse, my dad. *Ugh. Get it together, Philippian.* The consequences were adding up as quickly as time was slipping away.

I gripped my pencil and stared at the words on the paper, forcing myself to focus. At least I was trying to.

~ *10* ~

"Um ... we are sss ... sss ... supposed to sss ... sss ... study together now." I was right back where I had started. Nervous. Anxious. Stuttering. *We* were right back where we had started. Strangers.

Izzy opened her science journal to the page with "Science Project" written at the top in her perfect cursive writing. She scooted her chair closer to mine. "We have to whisper, remember" she said. *I remembered.*

Her voice trembled the same way my mom's voice shook anytime she had been crying but tried pretending she hadn't. Izzy didn't look like she had been crying. She looked as beautiful as ever. And she smelled good. Like strawberries. Like strawberry shortcake. Sitting next to her made my stomach growl like an angry bear defending its young.

"I have some ideas for the project, if you want to hear them," she whispered.

If? Of course I wanted to hear them. I wanted to hear anything Izzy had to say. I wanted to ask her why she had not spoken to me since the night she left my house. Why she had decided to stop being my friend. I wanted to ask what was wrong today. All I could do was listen.

"You like insects," she said, "and you're good with them."

Like? That was putting it mildly.

"I was thinking we could design a butterfly garden and injured insect sanctuary here at the school. Maybe beside the cafeteria, in the unused space." She raised her eyes. For the first time in a long time, she looked at me.

Mom always told me I am the smartest eleven year old she has ever met, but I think Izzy might be smarter than me. Of course, I was almost twelve.

"What do you think?" she asked.

"Yeah ... Yes! It's mmm ... mmm ... mmm," I stuttered.

"Awesome," she said at the same time, completing my thought. I nodded. She made some notes in her journal and looked up again. "So I guess this means we are going to have to get together to work on this."

She must have been reading my mind. I wanted to jump with excitement. I didn't. Before I had a chance to chime in on the details, Izzy continued with her own plans. "We will have to meet here. My dad says I can't go back to your house."

My dreams deflated like the air escaping a runaway balloon. My chin suddenly dropping to my chest must have been a dead giveaway.

"I'm sorry, Philippian. I am. My dad isn't comfortable with me being at your house anymore."

"I'll talk to him. I'll apologize. I nnn ... nnn ... never meant to worry anyone. I knnn ... knnn ... knnn ... know he's mad and I don't blame him. But I'll go talk to him." I wanted to make things right. I wanted to fix this so she could be my friend again.

"It isn't about the trail, Philippian, or about us getting back late. It's more. I've tried talking to him about it. He won't listen to me. I know he won't listen to you either." It was more than she had said to me in weeks. It wasn't what I wanted to hear, but at least she was talking.

"What is it?"

"It's your name. It's what your name means."

I didn't know where to go from there. No one had ever had a problem with my name. And what was wrong with it anyway?

Before I could think to ask more about her dad's problem with my name, Mrs. Walla began handing out the graded quizzes. My immediate future hung on the results of that quiz. The quiz I'd fumbled through. The quiz I barely remembered taking.

There were groans and cheers as the quizzes hit the tables. Mrs. Walla kept a straight face with each one. Then she got to me. I studied her face, trying to read either disappointment or pride in her eyes. I saw neither.

She placed my quiz face down on my desk, as she had done for everyone else. The blood rushed through my veins. My hands shook like a bad case of Parkinson's. There was no turning back. I gulped down a mouthful of air and clenched my teeth. With my thumb and finger barely half an inch apart, I turned the paper over.

Seventy-two? Ugh. Sure, it was passing, by a mere two points, but it was still a passing grade. I could argue that point when I showed it to my mom after school. I already knew what she would say. "Seventy-two is not passing in the Macedon household."

Grounded! My new middle name. Philippian Grounded Macedon. Yep, it would suit me. I was never going to see the light of day again. At least not until I made a better grade on the next Friday quiz. My weekend was officially blown. I smacked myself in the forehead with a clammy palm. "There is no one to blame but yourself," my dad had said to me a million times. Now I knew what he meant.

"We will need to plan our study time here at school," Izzy interrupted my pity party. She must have done well enough, seeing as how she didn't seem concerned at all about her weekend. I had never had a weekend to worry about until now ... and now it was ruined.

"Lunch time?" It was the only time we could work on it, unless we both got to school early or stayed late.

Izzy nodded. "I suppose. We need to design the garden and then take it to the principal to make sure we can do it. The project is due in May. That is the perfect time to move the plants."

She had thought of everything. She wasn't even the one who liked insects so much, and she had already put so much thought into this project. I hadn't given it a second thought. There was still time. Plenty of time.

"You're pretty smart, you know." I was sure she would laugh and stop being so serious. No such luck. I think I must have made her feel worse, because she lowered her eyes and her bottom lip quivered.

"We just have to get a good grade," she said, putting all her things into her backpack. The bell rang, telling us to move on to the next class.

"Monday at lunch; work on what plants we will need over the weekend."

She never looked back or waited for me to say anything. She ran out the door and vanished into the sea of students.

Angst of the Middle-school Newbie

~ *11* ~

Jared smacked me in the back of the head when I walked through the kitchen door. "Took you long enough to get home, Philly-Willy. You must have bad news." He waved his Friday quizzes in the air and danced in circles. "I made all A's. Nana-nana-boo-boo!"

I tried to slip by him. "*Ignore him. He'll go away,*" everyone told me. He never did.

"Where are your quizzes? I bet you didn't make A's like me," he pointed and laughed. He was right. He always did better than me. He was better than me at everything. School. Sports. Friends. He had it all. Looks. Height. He was tall. Strong. Smart. Fast. He was everything I wasn't, and everyone loved him for it.

But at home, I knew Mom and Dad loved me, too. It might be the only place anyone cared about me, but at least they did. A few bad grades wouldn't change that. I hoped.

He hooked his big arm around my neck and pushed his knuckles into my scalp. He drug them back and forth, until I was sure my head would explode and my hair looked like a wild wounded animal. When he finally let me go, I wanted to run to my room and bury my face in my bed for the entire weekend.

"What's going on in here with you boys?" Mom appeared out of nowhere. She took one look at my hair and turned her attention to Jared. "Could you please leave your little brother alone?"

"See, Philippian, even Mom thinks you're little," Jared snickered.

"I do not. Stop it." Mom wagged her finger in front of his nose, giving Jared a non-verbal warning of the consequences he would face if he didn't back down. Most of the time, that's all it took.

"Look, Mom. I made all A's." Jared flashed his quizzes, knowing what would happen next.

"Nice job as always, Jared." She scanned his grades, smiling. Then she turned to me. "And yours," she asked. I hung my head and handed over my one grade. My seventy-two. I waited, just as Jared did, for the outcry of shame.

"What happened, Philip?" Mom wasn't a yeller, but I expected her to be one when she saw my grade. Instead, it was as if she was worried about me.

"What happened? Really?" Jared did enough yelling for both of them. "What happened is he bombed the test! Aren't you going to scream? Ground him? Something?" He threw his hands in the air and demanded justice.

"So, Philip, what happened today? This isn't like you. You usually pull an eighty at least. You know seventy-two isn't passing in the Macedon household."

"I know, Mom. But right before the quiz," I stopped. I wanted Jared to leave before I shared the details of my day. The last thing I wanted was give him more ammo to use against me. If looks could kill, he would have dropped dead right there in the kitchen from the daggers I threw straight through his heart of stone. But they don't ... and he didn't.

"Mom, please," I needed a little help in the privacy department. Mom finally took the hint and turned to Jared.

"Get out of here," she said, smacking her hands together. "Now."

Once he was gone, though I was sure he was lurking down the hallway listening, I continued. "Right before Mrs. Walla handed out the quiz Izzy spoke to me for the first time since the night we walked down the trail. She spoke to me and said she would talk to me later. It was all I could think about the whole time."

I waited for her to laugh, to tell me I was too young to be worrying about what a girl said to me. She would be right. I knew it. Although I was almost twelve years old, to her, I was still just a little boy. I guess it's hard for moms to let their sons grow up. But there I was, on the edge of manhood, with months standing in the way. Soon I would be a pre-teen, and that would make me a man!

Of course, it didn't change the seventy-two or help it at all. All I could do now was throw myself at the mercy of the court and pray she was the romantic I believed her to be.

"Yeah, you're grounded."

She took no time to consider the facts or my feelings. The jury was in, and I was guilty. I wanted to scream, to make her hear my case, to demand to be heard. I wanted to make her understand how hurt I have been since Izzy stopped talking to me. To explain how knowing she was talking to me again threw me way off my game. I also wanted to cry. To stomp my feet. To throw the biggest temper tantrum known to man. If I did any of the things running through my mind, my dad would no doubt come straight home and give me the beating of a lifetime. So, instead of doing any of these things, I tucked my tail between my legs and accepted the ruling like a man.

"I'm just kidding," she said, followed by a rolling thunder of laughter. "I want to see it improve next week. You're allowed one mishap every now and then, as long as it isn't too serious. This isn't so serious." She wrapped her arms around me and pulled me close. All of a sudden, I could tell. Yep, she's pregnant.

I pushed away and looked at her. Her cheeks were so pretty. Prettier than I had ever seen them before. My mom is the most beautiful woman in the world, but suddenly she looked even more beautiful. I noticed a tiny round belly she had never had before. Yep, I was going to be a big brother, and it was starting to sound pretty cool.

"Hey, I got invited to a friend's house today," I said before she changed her mind. "He's so super cool, Mom. He has a python!"

Her eyes widened. "Python?"

"He's shorter than me, too. Can I go, Mom? Can I go? Please? I promise I'll bring my quiz grade up next week. I won't let you down. Please, Mom. Please?"

I don't know if she was more surprised over the python or me having a friend, finally. Maybe it's because there is someone alive who is shorter than me.

"Who is this friend? Where does he live? Do you have his parents' names and number?"

"Wow, Mom. Well, his name is Michael Donavon Schmitzer." I filled her in on all the details, and assured her what time I would be home. I had never gone to a friend's house before. My insides twisted like a roller coaster. With a nod, Mom agreed to let me go. I packed Faith-Grace in her travel container and positioned her safely in the basket on my bike. Off we rode.

It was the best day of my whole life!

Best day ever!

Angst of the Middle-school Newbie

~ *12*~

I stood on the step, admiring the artistic stones around Michael's door. His house was huge compared to mine. Ginormous. He even had a big gold knocker for those tall people who didn't want to use the doorbell. I would never be able to bang on the door with that thing. I didn't care. Michael wouldn't be able to either.

I tucked Faith-Grace in the side pocket of my survival pack and pressed the doorbell to let him know I had finally arrived. The chimes rang for so long I thought no one was ever going to answer the door.

What if it was a joke? What if Michael wasn't really my friend? What if everything Jared had said about me was true? What if ...

The door swung open. Michael smiled and waved me in. "Hey, Phil, come on in. I'll introduce you to my python, Akeyra. You can even hold her if you want." His house smelled like cinnamon or apple pie. I couldn't be sure. It reminded me that I had missed lunch.

The ceilings were so high my whole house could have fit right there in his living room. There were a million windows. I would hate to have to wash those every other Saturday, like we do at my house. The dining room table had enough chairs for two or three families.

"Wow! How many brothers and sisters do you have?" I had to laugh when my own voice echoed.

"One of each. I'm in the middle," he said. *All this, and only three of them.* "Want to get a bite before we go to my room," he asked, leading me to the fridge.

I stopped when we got to the kitchen. I had never seen a kitchen so big. There were two ovens. Two. Like one wasn't enough. And an island in the middle of the kitchen so large it had enough appliances to be its own kitchen.

"Want a snack? Something to drink?" He was already filling his arms with food and drinks before I could even respond. I nodded and he added more to his stash. "Come on; let's go play some games or something."

"You're taking that to your room?" I wasn't about to get into trouble at his house. I got into enough at my own. There's no way my mom would allow me to eat in my room, especially all the stuff he had.

"Sure, why not," he asked as he slammed the refrigerator door shut with his foot. "My folks don't mind. Besides, the maid will clean it up later."

"You have a ... maid?" I couldn't stop myself from asking. The words spilled right out of my lips before I could suck them back in.

"No. We have three. This house isn't going to clean itself." He laughed and shoved a handful of Doritos into his mouth.

I followed Michael up the winding staircase. We passed seven bedrooms and three bathrooms before we got to his room at the end of the hallway.

"I got the best one!" He raised his eyebrows and nodded his head. "Wait 'til you see this." He pushed the door with his elbow, and the door flung open.

"Oh ... my ... goodness!" I had never seen anything like it. I thought *my* house was big. His room was bigger than mine and Jared's put together. I stood in the middle of the room, trying to see everything from one spot. There was a flat-screen television on the wall, looking like something out of a movie theater. And the games. Wow. The games. There must have been a few hundred of them. I didn't even know that many existed.

Michael opened his arms and all the snacks landed on his bed. His king-size bed. *Why does a kid his size need a bed so big*? I shook my head, forcing out the negative thoughts about my new friend.

"And here's Akeyra. She's a Ball Python." He pulled a string on the wall and two heavy drapes rolled back, revealing a glass wall that spread the entire length and height of his room. Inside was a snake so long it almost reached each end of the container. She was a beautiful black snake, with brown spots trimmed in black and white. Her container was like something out of a zoo magazine with full-size, live trees, a small pond, and a cave. All in his *bedroom*.

My stomach was in my throat, making it hard to swallow. Trying not to make any sudden movements, I unzipped my survival pack and pulled out my inhaler. I shook it a few times before pushing it between my lips and sucking in the medicine. The whole time, I never took my eyes off the snake. Not once.

Michael cracked a smile and chuckled. "Relax, Phil. There's nothing to be afraid of. I've had Akeyra since she was just a baby. You should have seen her then." He spread his hands out wide enough to fit a shoe box. "She was only about this big when she was born."

"How old is she now?" I had to sit down. The room spun around and, for a minute, everything was getting dark. I felt better sitting on his bed.

"She's about three years old now." He opened a smaller aquarium and stuck his hand so far down it disappeared. A few minutes later, he pulled out his hand, holding a big, squirming, white rat.

I'm sure the rat looked at me, begging me to save him. He must have known what his future held. I'm guessing he'd watched many of his family members go through the same trauma. I wanted to save him. I did. But it was the nature of the beast, and the food chain demands order. Michael opened a window in the large glass container and dangled the rat in the air, its feet clawing at his hand to get away.

Akeyra must have known it was feeding time. She coiled up tight and waited to accept the rat. As soon as Michael dropped it, Akeyra wrapped herself around the rat and squeezed tight until it stopped moving. Then she swallowed it whole. I watched as the whole rat moved along the snake's body, being digested.

Part of me thought for sure I would be sick. The other part of me was fascinated. I had always loved reptiles, but I had never before seen any reptile so large and so close up. I had a million questions.

How often does Akeyra eat? How long will she live? How do you know she's ready to shed and how often will she shed? When will she have babies? Could you have more than one in the same container? Why is she called a Ball Python? Is she the only kind of Ball Python or are there many types? The questions ran through my mind like a marathon runner headed towards the finish line.

It was the best day of my life, and Michael was my new best friend ... the only best friend I ever had.

"Michael," I said, grabbing a hand full of Doritos and opening a can of Dr. Pepper.

"Yeah, Phil?"

I shoved the Doritos into my mouth and closed my fingers up inside my hand. I held my fist out. Topping off the best day of my life was my first ever fist pump.

Yeah, me and Michael are going to be good friends for a long, long time.

~ *13* ~

Dear Jesus, it's me, Philippian Macedon from 222 Carthage Road. I'm sorry I haven't talked to You in a while but I have so much to tell You. I have a new friend. He's my best friend. You should see his house. It is huge! Anyway, the reason I needed to talk to You this morning is because today Izzy wants me to spend my lunch time with her so we can do the science project stuff. Jesus, could You please make her want to be my friend again? Then I could have two friends!

I'm scared, Jesus. What if she doesn't want to be my friend again? What if she doesn't like the stuff I did for the science project? Mom says I'm the smartest eleven year-old she knows but what if I'm not smart enough to make a good grade on the project and Izzy gets mad at me all over again?

Jesus, I don't know what to do. Could You please help me?

That's all.

Oh, and if you talk to my dad today, could You tell him I love him all the way around the world two times and back again? Thank You. Amen.

Today started out like any other day. I got dressed and ate breakfast. Jared called me names and punched me in the arm. The neighborhood kids picked on me and called me a sissy because of my girl's bike. Most of the kids ignored me in the hallway. Yep, it was a normal day like any other.

That was until Vicky Smith, the biggest, meanest seventh grader in the whole school decided today was the day she was going to introduce herself to me ... personally.

I saw her coming. She looked right at me. Her nostrils were so big I could see all the way to her brain. Her arms were straight down by her side, but her hands were balled up. The ground shook when she stomped down the hallway. Kids moved to each side of the hallway, as if she were parting the Red Sea. She was coming for me.

Right then, I would have been thankful to be stuffed inside an old smelly locker. At least then I could have hidden from the wrath of this highly-feared seventh grader.

Vicky Smith was even bigger than Jared, and probably meaner. Her hair was as short as Jared's, but big and super curly. It was so big and curly it looked more like a dark brown football helmet.

Blood pumped through every vein in my body so fast I was sure I had just completed a full triathlon with the fastest time. My knees smacked against each other. Sweat soaked my arm pits. The Lucky Charms I had for breakfast were climbing up my throat and ready to decorate the walls. *I'm about to be a goner*!

I searched the crowd for Jared. He would help me. I knew he would! Right? Michael? Anyone?

Vicky Smith shoved through the few remaining terrified kids, never once taking her eyes off me. Just like in the movies, my whole life flashed before my eyes like a poorly-produced short film. There was nowhere to run. No one to hide behind. It was time to meet my Maker. I dug for my inhaler, not even attempting to hide it. I held on to it like a life line in a violent sea.

I had never fully appreciated how big Vicky Smith was until she was standing in my face, looking down on me. Her breath was warm against my face, like a fire-breathing dragon. The back of my neck burned instantly as I leaned way back to look up at her.

The hallway was silent. Not a sound. I suppose everyone was holding their breath just as I was. Everyone except Vicky Smith. She dug one fist in her hip and waved the other in my face. Her fist was so tight her knuckles had lost all color.

"I. Want. That. Bike," she demanded. Her crooked, yellow teeth were so big I wondered if she had been crossed with a crocodile. One snap would take my head off at the shoulders.

"I. Want. That. Bike," she repeated, pushing her fist closer to my glasses.

She wants my bike, I thought. *Who would ever want my bike?* Her dark brown eyes were as large as golf balls as she stared down my nose.

"I want it, and I'm taking it this afternoon!" She opened her fist and flicked the tip of my nose with her finger. With that, she spun on the heels of her black, fully-laced combat boots and stomped down the seventh grade hallway, disappearing beyond the sea of amused faces.

The bell rang and everyone scattered like rats on a sinking ship. I was left standing alone in an empty hallway, wondering how *my* bike had become the object of Vicky Smith's desire without warning. Vicky Smith, world-famous middle-school-bully. Vicky Smith, tom-boy-*ish* over-sized Neanderthal suddenly had some odd desire to ride *my* girly pink bicycle with a white flower basket and bright sparkly pink seat. I could imagine Jared wanting to ride my bike long before I would Vicky Smith. But Vicky Smith wanted my bike, and I was pretty sure she was willing to do whatever it took to take it from me.

Angst of the Middle-school Newbie

~ *14* ~

Izzy was waiting exactly where she told me she would be. No surprise there. I had been so excited over the weekend, knowing I would not only see her but talk to her today as well. Vicky Smith ruined that for me. I had thought of little else all day except her attack and demands.

Izzy held her science journal close to her body, arms folded against her chest. She was facing the sun, so she squinted her eyes, watching me walk across the newly-mowed school lawn.

"This looks like a great spot here," she said, turning in a full circle. "We could even put up a pretty fence to enclose it." She handed me a sheet of paper with a lot of writing on the front, and drawings on the back.

"These are all great ideas, bbb ... bbb ... bbb ... but, how are we going to ppp ... ppp ... ppp ... pay for it?"

She handed me another piece of paper. *I should have known she had already thought of the finances.* "We will ask for donations," she announced. "We can make fliers, write letters, and go to the school board meeting."

I could hear the rocks in my empty head rattling around when I thought of all the work involved ... *for a grade.* A science grade, no less. I liked science as much as the next sixth- grader but this was going way overboard.

I dug the toes of my tennis shoes into the ground, disrupting a small patch of bright green grass. I started to complain, to tell her I didn't want to do so much for a project. I wanted to say, "Let's make a volcano or something," but I didn't. I didn't because it hit me like a line-drive right between my big square glasses. The more work there was to be done, the more time I would get with Izzy, the prettiest girl in the whole sixth grade.

"Did you make a list of butterfly plants we can put in the garden? What about some kind of built-in safe place for injured insects? Did you do any of those things over the weekend?"

I slid my hand in my back pocket and pulled out a wrinkled piece of paper. My own research. When I handed it to her, she rolled her eyes and blew out a deep breath.

"How long are you going to be mad at me, Izzy? I said I'm sorry."

Izzy's shoulders dropped. "I'm not mad at you, Philippian. My dad says I can't be friends with you, though."

"Because of my name? That makes no sense!" Of all the things I had been picked on in my life, my name had never been one of them. I was proud of my name. Proud of what it meant and how my parents chose it.

"My dad says your parents are religious fanatics and I can't be friends with you."

I didn't know how to respond. In all my nine ... almost twelve years of life, I had never had anyone dislike my name or not want to be my friend because my family loves Jesus. All this time, I thought everyone loved Jesus.

"I'll work on the terrarium and plants. You can work on the other, if you like," I said. I didn't wait for a response, and I didn't spend my whole lunch time with her. I felt like I had been punched in the stomach by Vicky Smith. I walked away and left Izzy standing alone, something I never thought I would do.

I wish my dad was here. He would know what to do. He would know what to say.

The rest of the day was painful. Suddenly everyone wanted to speak to me in the hallway ... well, they wanted to point at me and laugh about how Vicky Smith was going to beat me up and take my bike. I looked everywhere for Michael, my best friend. The only good part of my day ... ever. It wasn't like him to miss school. He would be on my side for sure, even if he was shorter and smaller than me. He would never let me face Vicky Smith alone. Not the way Jared was going to do.

I watched the hands on the clock drag by, but they also seemed to fly. I wanted it over, but I didn't want to face Vicky Smith. I must have been daydreaming again because Mrs. Walla had that same disappointed look on her face that meant after-school detention. When everyone else filed out of the room to go to their next class, Mrs. Walla curled her finger and called me to the front of the desk for a pow-wow.

Great! What else could possibly go wrong today?

Mrs. Walla sat on the edge of her desk and pointed for me to sit at the front table. She crossed her ankles and let them swing. She waited to speak like she had to swirl her thoughts around in her head first. So I waited with her.

"Mr. Macedon, I heard about your run-in this morning with Miss Smith." She gestured with her hands like she wanted me to fill her in, and then dropped them in her lap. I nodded. It wasn't like there was anything to add. She knew what had happened. She knew I had no defense.

"Can I give you a bit of advice?"

I had to stop her right there. "Am I in trouble?"

Mrs. Walla let out a tiny snort. She flicked her wrist and shook her head. "Oh, no, dear. I just wanted to talk to you for a bit. I'll give you a note for your next class. It's my planning period, and I felt like you could use a friend right now."

She had no idea. The only friend I had was missing-in-action. My brother was a no-show and Izzy didn't like my name. Heck, yeah, I needed a friend in the worst way! I moved to the edge of my seat and waited for her words of wisdom on how to defeat the great Vicky Smith! Surely Mrs. Walla was going to give me some tips from a girl's point of view.

"You need to know one thing, Mr. Macedon. God has not given you a spirit of fear but a spirit of peace. He tells us 365 times in His word that we don't need to fear anything. Including Miss Smith. He created you to be a conqueror, not frightened."

"Mrs. Walla," my voice vibrated. So did my lips. "Have you seen the size of that girl compared to me? She's a giant. I am almost the smallest kid in this whole school."

"Have you heard the story of David and Goliath?" Her forehead wrinkled.

"So what do I do? She's a girl! Even if I was big enough, I can't hit a girl. And she's definitely going to hit me."

"What you do is remember that you can do all things through Christ who gives you strength ... Philippian!"

I looked down at the bracelet my dad had given me. I guess I'd known it all along, but I wasn't really sure what to do about it. Sure, my bracelet says that, but I don't think Jesus meant I would be able to defend myself against such a bully.

"Mr. Macedon, broken people do broken things. You may very well be the only Jesus she ever sees. Do you really like that pink bike?"

"No ma'am, but it's the only one my parents could afford. I ride it to school. I'm supposed to get a new one for my birthday ... hopefully."

"This afternoon, when Miss Smith is waiting on you, and surely she will be, I want you to remember who you are in Christ. It's a heavy weight to carry at eleven years-old ... I know."

"I'm almost twelve. Pre-teen," I informed her.

"Okay, twelve. Even still, it's a heavy weight to carry to be the light of the world. But that's what you've been called to do. Perhaps, instead of showing Miss Smith that you are afraid of her, you should show her that you care about her. You never know. You may be the only person to ever care about her." Miss Walla scribbled on a half sheet of paper and signed her name at the bottom. "Just my two cents worth. Now, get to class." She handed me the note and smiled the same way my mom does when she's proud of me.

I took the note and nodded. I wasn't sure how I would handle the confrontation after school, but at least I didn't feel so alone anymore.

"Oh, and Mr. Macedon," Mrs. Walla called after me. I turned back to look at her again. "I'll be praying for you this afternoon. I pray for you every day."

The clock marched on.

~ *15* ~

The crowd had gathered around my pink bike. They were foaming at the mouth like hungry pythons waiting to squeeze the life and blood out of their weekly squirming rat.

Vicky Smith had wasted no time making her appearance. Her fists were still tight and her nostrils still enormous. She had no intention of leaving school any other way than on my bike.

Still no sign of Jared or Michael. Not even Izzy was there to stand by me. No one was there to stand up for me or defend me. No one. I watched as the swarm of hungry students waited for my arrival. I'm sure they saw me, because, as soon as they did, they got louder, screaming for a fight.

Dear Jesus, it's me, Philippian Macedon from 222 Carthage Road. I'm at school now, though. I really need some help. She's going to hurt me. I know it. She's going to hurt me and take my bike and everyone else will have something else to laugh at me about.

Mrs. Walla said I don't have to be afraid of anyone or anything. I don't know how true that is because I am very afraid right now. No one is here to help me. Is it too much to ask that You help me? Please. Thank You, and Amen.

I walked as slowly as I could, barely moving my feet along the sidewalk to the bike rack. My knees smashed against each other with every step. My teeth clanked together so hard my jaws hurt. I wiped my sweating palms on my shorts and moved forward with more fear than any eleven year-old should ever know, or even a twelve year-old for that matter.

As I made my way closer, Vicky Smith slammed her fist in her other hand. "Told you! I'm taking your bike." She wrapped her hands around the handlebars of my bike and yanked it, trying to free it from the rack.

"Th ... th ... there's a lock on it."

Vicky Smith spotted the key hanging on a chain around my neck and, before I could tuck it into my shirt, she ripped it from me, leaving my neck burning. She unlocked the bike and tossed the rubber-coated chain and padlock to the ground. She stuck out her tongue and blew a mouthful of spit in the air, making a motor-boating sound that everyone else found hilarious.

She threw one leg over the middle bar and rested herself on the pink sparkly seat. Then ... then she smiled. I don't think I have ever seen Vicky Smith smile before. It was a creepy, I-told-you-so kind of smile, but it was a smile.

The crowd of satisfied students stepped aside and made a clearing for her to ride away on my bike. *My* bike. Even if it was a girl's bike, it was *my* bike.

With one foot on a pedal and the other on the ground, Vicky Smith was proud of her accomplishment. She had done what she'd set out to do and with little to no interference.

Then, without warning, she planted both feet on the ground and looked back at me over her shoulder. The muscles in her jaws relaxed. Her nostrils returned to a normal size. The wrinkles left her forehead. She wasn't angry anymore and she wasn't happy. There was no smile. She wasn't even laughing. With her head cocked to one side, Vicky Smith had gone from being determined to take me down to being confused as to why it was so easy to do it.

"Why, Macedon?" Her voice rattled. "Why would you just stand there and let me take your bike?"

A heckler from the crowd chimed in, "Wasn't like he could take you anyway." Several others joined in the fun.

I shrugged my shoulders. What could I do, really? She was going to take it one way or the other. No reason to get pummeled in the process.

Vicky Smith threw her leg over the bike and smacked the kickstand with her boot. "Seriously? Why?"

"You seem to need it more than I do. And if that's true, then I'm happy to give it to you. I hope you enjoy it."

I was shocked by own lack of fear. Apparently so was Vicky Smith. She had been used to instilling fear among kids younger and smaller than her for many years. I wasn't her first and would probably not be her last.

I did not give you a spirit of fear, but one of peace and love.

I tried to swallow the lump in my throat, but it wouldn't move. Vicky Smith hung her head. After a few minutes that seemed more like an eternity, she looked up at me.

"No one has ever been nice to me. I don't want your bike." She picked up the chain and lock and handed them to me.

I held up my hands, refusing to take them from her. "It's okay," I said. "I want you to have it. I've been wanting a black one anyway."

She smiled. A real smile. With tiny crinkles around her eyes and everything. It had to be a world record. Vicky Smith smiling. A real, true, honest-to-goodness smile.

She shook her head and rode away on my ... on *her* bike. I had a warm feeling inside as I watched her move down the dirt gravel road away from school. The dust settled and soon I was standing there all alone again, except I didn't feel so alone anymore.

"Need a ride?" Out of nowhere, Mrs. Walla pulled up beside me in her car. Leaning out the window, she asked again, "You need a ride home?" I had to laugh. She knew what had happened. She knew how I was going to respond to the school bully even before I did. And she knew I had just given up my only way of getting home.

I nodded. What else was there to do?

"Hop in." We laughed all the way to my house. I had defeated my giant.

~ 16 ~

Worry had settled in for the stay. Days had passed, and I had heard nothing from Michael. *I bet he was swallowed by his python*, I thought more than once. My mom won't let me go to his house without talking to him first.

"It's rude," she said. "You don't just show up at someone's house."

So all I could do was wait. Every day I waited. I waited for him to call. Waited for him to stop by. Waited for him to show up at school. None of these things happened. I had prayed for him to come back. Nothing. So, yeah, I was worried.

I didn't have the best of luck with the few friends I had found. Well, two, really, and already I was down to one. Things were not looking good for me. They never had in the first place. For once, I thought my luck was changing. That's what I got for thinking.

Three things had happened since I started school. Izzy had become my friend, and then decided she couldn't be my friend anymore. Michael had introduced himself and invited me over, then disappeared. And Vicky Smith had turned over a new leaf. I was the common denominator.

I was the reason Izzy didn't want to be friends, or at least my name was the reason. I was the reason Vicky Smith turned over a new leaf. It was looking like I would be the reason for the disappearance of Michael. The hair on the back of my neck stood straight up as the image of a dark murder mystery flashed in front of my glasses. I would no doubt be the number one suspect. I had always wanted to play the leading role in a major motion picture. Especially a thriller ... but not like this. Not with Michael as the victim.

Other than those three things, everything else was pretty much the same as it had been my whole life.

Mom had been taking me back and forth to school, usually stopping for breakfast in the mornings, which gave us more time to talk without

Jared butting into the conversation. I was learning more about babies, pregnancy, and life in general. I am almost twelve, so I knew most of it already. I learned a lot in science class, and a lot more in the lunchroom, just by listening to the other kids talking around me. So Mom didn't have to explain too much to me. I was glad, too, because it wasn't something I wanted to talk to her about. Just thinking about it makes my stomach flip-flop.

Since we still had not heard from Dad, he still didn't know about the new baby on the way. "I bet he will be excited," I told Mom. My dad loves kids, and having another one would probably make him so happy he would never want to leave us again. At least that's what I had been praying for.

"Do you think it's a girl or a boy," I asked Mom one morning on the way to school. She shrugged her shoulders just once, so I knew she wasn't sure yet. Maybe she wanted to wait until Dad got home to find out what the baby was, if he made it back in time at all.

Then she asked me, "Do you want a little sister or a little brother?" I had spent a lot of time thinking about it. At first I thought it wouldn't matter. I was going to be the middle child either way, and nothing would be fun about it. But then I got to thinking ... *I will get to be the big brother for a change.* Once I realized this valuable piece of information, I started making a list of the things I wanted to teach my little brother or sister, and all the things I wanted to do with him or her.

"A brother! I definitely want a little brother!" And according to my mom's doctor, the baby should be born at the end of June, not too far away from my birthday. *It would be so cool if we had the same birthday.* At least if I had a little brother, I would be sure to have a friend who would stay forever. Since I would be the big brother and be nice to him, he would always be my best friend. Yeah, a brother. That's what I had been praying for.

We talked about other things, too, like Izzy, and my new best friend, Michael. Mom hadn't asked a lot about either of them, but probably because I hadn't brought it up yet. But, this morning on the way to school, I did.

"We work on our project at lunch, so she speaks to me then," I began.

"And how's the project coming along?" Mom kept her eyes on the road while she talked. She was the most careful driver I knew.

"Okay, I guess. I have all the butterfly plants growing from seeds. They are in my closet for now."

"Oh, yeah? When do you plant them in the garden?" My mom was actually interested. No one had ever been interested in my hobbies.

"The project is due at the end of May, the perfect time to relocate them. The last frost should have come and gone, and warmer weather should be here to stay. So, it will work."

"And the donations? How are they coming along?"

Ugh, donations. I hated the thought of asking for money. Thankfully, so far, I hadn't had to. I blew out a long deep breath. "Slowly. Izzy seems to think they will pick up soon. She says everyone is recovering from Christmas still."

"I bet it's going to beautiful. Are you both presenting, or are you going to let her do all the speaking?"

My mom knew me well. She knew how nervous I got in public, and how badly I stuttered when speaking out loud. I hadn't decided, and Izzy hadn't brought it up.

"I don't think I can do it. I just want to do the physical stuff. She is better at speaking. I'll just let her take it from there."

Mom stopped at the light and, for the first time on our morning drive, she looked at me. "Do you think that's fair? Isn't Izzy doing a lot of the physical work, too? I know she's doing a lot of the leg work for donations. Shouldn't you share all the work, not only the parts you are comfortable with?"

I slapped my forehead.

"I know how much you hate talking in public. It doesn't mean you shouldn't," she added. She pulled into the car-rider line up. A long line of cars waited in front of us, and we moved slower than a snail crossing the interstate.

"I can't, Mom. I just can't."

She held the wheel with both hands and looked at me again. "Philip, you know better. You can do all things! All things through Christ who gives you strength. You have to remember this. You have to hold on to it. You see, God cares about every detail of your life, big and small. He cares that you are hurting over losing a friend. He cares that you are worried about Michael. And he cares that you fear speaking in public. Because He cares, you don't ever have to handle any of these situations alone. Instead of running from difficult parts of your life, you should embrace them, knowing that God has your best interests at heart."

I had nothing to add. I loved our talks, but sometimes I wanted to talk without it turning into a life lesson, and my mom could turn anything in a life lesson.

Finally it was my turn to get out. "Love you, Mom," I said, and darted out of car without giving her a chance at a last-second lecture.

~ *17* ~

The bell between first and second period rang as always, rattling the large windows in math class. I put most of my things into my backpack and carried the rest under my arm. I kept my head down as usual while making my way through the crowd.

"Hey, Phil!" His voice was so loud it was hard to believe it came from such a small guy.

"Michael! Where have you been, dude?" We shook hands like old men. I had never been happier in my whole life. I still had one friend. My best friend.

"I'll tell you later. Come over tonight?" He waved and faded into the circus of familiar, nameless faces.

He was alive. He was okay. Christmas morning couldn't have been better. I wouldn't be starring in my own thriller, but Michael Donavon Schmitzer was alive and well. There could be no greater news.

But then there was.

Science class had not started. Everyone was busy taking their seats and catching up on any gossip that may have occurred between classes. Izzy tossed her bag onto the floor between our table and the window. She scooted right up next to me and spun my chair around until we were facing each other. I wanted to vomit right there. To spew all of my breakfast burrito in her lap. I didn't really want to but I was sure I was about to. The stern look on her face made me think I was about to be on restriction for life ... as my mom would do if I ever had to have the cops search for me again.

"Do you think I could go to church with you sometime?"

"Ch ... ch ... church? Seriously?" She hadn't spoken to me outside of our lunch business meetings for weeks and now *church*? "Your dad is never going to allow th ... th ... that."

"No, but my mom will. And I want to go. I want to know more about it." Her voice was sparkly. So were her big beautiful blue eyes.

"Have you ever been to church?"

She shook her head and looked away.

"I'm sorry, Izzy," I said. I touched the top of her hand only to make her feel better. I was careful not to touch her fingers at all. That would have been awkward. "I didn't mean to upset you. Sure you can come with me Sunday, if you'd like."

She nodded, smiled, and moved her chair back to her spot at our table. This day was definitely turning out to be the second-best day ever!

By the time Mom picked me up after school, I was bursting to tell her everything that had happened. I was so excited I didn't even know what to share first. So I picked a topic and ran with it.

"Mom! You won't believe my day. It was so awesome!" I could hardly get a breath out, I was so excited. "Michael's alive and wants me to come over. Izzy wants to go to church! Do you believe it? She wants to go to church ... with *me*! Man, God really does hear our prayers. Well, at least He heard mine. I mean, I was ..."

"Philip," she gripped my hand, "take a deep breath. One bit of information at a time."

I sucked in all the air I could get in my cheeks and counted to seven before letting it out. I tried holding it to the count of ten, but I couldn't make it that long. So after seven death-defying seconds, I made my big announcement.

"I have two friends. Not one, but *two*!" I was bouncing so much in the front seat I almost forgot to buckle my seat belt, but, of course, my mom refused to move the car until I did. As soon I clicked my belt in place, I continued. "Two friends, Mom. Can you believe it? *Me*! I sure wish Dad was here so I could tell him."

"That's great, Sweetie. I am happy you have made friends. I knew you would."

"So can I go tonight," I begged. I hadn't been to Michael's house in forever. I couldn't wait to see his python again, and maybe even get to feed it this time. "Can I? Please? Please?" I had my hands folded together and my bottom lip out as far as I could stick it. That always works.

Mom nodded, but I could tell something was going on. She winked and gave a crooked smile. *Yeah, something's going on.* "Can you drop me off on the way home? I don't want to waste a minute. It's been forever since we got to hang out."

"No, I think we should stop by the house first."

"But, Mom, I..."

"Philip, we need to stop by the house." Her happy, playful voice turned serious, and I knew not to say another word. The rest of the ride was silent, but inside my heart was bouncing like a trampoline.

As we pulled into the driveway, Mom said, "By the way, something came for you today."

"What's that mean," I asked, breaking my momentary vow of silence.

"Just what I said. Something came for you today. Something was delivered to the house with your name on it."

Nothing had ever come to our house with 'Philippian Macedon' written on it. Not a single piece of paper or anything.

"What is it? Who's it from?" The thoughts and images bolted through my head. Could this day get any better?

"I don't know who it's from, but it came with a note and I didn't peak at all." Then she pointed to the most amazing thing I had ever seen in all my eleven years and nine-months of life. More amazing than Izzy. My eyes had grown so large, I thought they were going to pop out of my head.

Sitting in our driveway, with a massive red bow right on top, was the greatest bicycle known to man! It was definitely the best bicycle at New Century Middle School, and I was going to be the envy of everyone. A bright red, Harley Davidson Road-master bicycle.

No one would ever pick on me again, at least not because of my bike.

The Red Road-master looked just like a real-life Harley Davidson motorcycle, complete with a fully-functioning speedometer and a leather seat built for two. A black, full-face helmet hung from the handlebars.

"Oh. My. Goodness," I screamed so loud I was pretty sure I wouldn't have a voice by dinner. I jumped up and down. I spun in circles. I was the king of the world.

It was the coolest bike I had ever seen. Cooler than any I had looked at or hoped for. Far cooler than any my parents were going to be able to afford for my twelfth birthday.

I had no clue who would have sent *me* such an amazing bike. I pulled the envelope off the handlebars and lifted the flap. There was a note inside.

When we seek God with our whole hearts and do as He calls us to do, He is faithful to give us the desires of our hearts. You are a conqueror and you have nothing to fear, ever.

Sincerely,

A proud observer.

I almost cried. Mom *did*. No one had ever cared about me before besides Mom and Dad. No one.

With my mom's permission, I saddled up, strapped on my helmet, and rode off into the great blue yonder to show my best friend in the whole wide world my brand new motorcycle bike.

~ *18* ~

I banged on the door with both my fists. I banged as hard as I could for as long as it took for someone to answer the door at Michael's house. I couldn't wait to show him. I was even going to let him ride it around the block if he wanted.

I continued to bang for what seemed like an hour, until a tall man opened the door and looked down to see who was knocking. The man was so tall and so skinny he looked like a piece of salt-water taffy being pulled at both ends. His scalp was way higher than his hair, and his eyes looked through me like a freshly-cleaned window on Saturday afternoon.

Am I at the wrong house? I thought.

"Are you Phil," the tall, skinny, bald man asked. His eyebrows scrunched together, and I couldn't tell if he was mad or curious. I nodded, squeezing my teeth together to keep them from chattering with fear.

"Come on in. Michael is expecting you." He stepped aside and held the door. I didn't know whether I should stand on my toes to try to reach his hand so I could shake it, or run for my life.

I ran.

I ran and never looked back. I ran all the way through the living room, up the winding staircase, and all the way down the hallway past all the other rooms.

My mouth was wide open while I sucked in as much air as I could with every breath. I bent over and rested my hands on my knees, trying to catch my breath so I could talk. I knocked on Michael's bedroom door and waited, still trying to get my breathing back on track without using my inhaler.

"Come on in, Phil," he called from his room. I slipped through the door, still gasping, only to find him wrapped up in blankets on his bed.

"It isn't even dark out," I said once I could breathe again. "What are you doing in bed? Come on, I have to show you something." I headed back to the door, but he stopped me.

"Phil, I can't," he said, not much higher than a weak whisper. His skin was a lot lighter than I remembered. Almost a light yellow. He must have picked up on my confusion because he started answering the questions that were floating around in my head.

"I'm sick, Phil. I have been for a while. That's why I was out for so long. The doctor says I might get better, but I will need to rest a lot." I stood at the end of his bed, staring at him. I didn't even know what to say, but it didn't stop the questions. *How sick is sick? When can you play? Am I going to get sick?*

"It isn't contagious," he said, reading my mind.

I wanted to change the subject, and he was more than happy to join me. We talked about his python, and he even let me feed her. I don't think I want to do that again anytime soon. I told him all about my bike, and we made plans to race once he felt better.

"So why do you have such a big house if you there are only three kids?" I had wanted to ask this since the first time I came over.

His belly shook when he chuckled. "You just haven't been here when we have a full house. My parents take in visiting pastors and missionaries when they come to town. That way, they aren't paying for a hotel and can have a nice place to rest, along with full-service cooking and cleaning." He took a few deep breaths and continued. "And there are times when they take in homeless people for a few nights during winter." For a second, he stopped talking and watched the sun sinking lower in the sky. "It was always my mom's dream."

"Wow," I interrupted. "Your parents are so nice. Was that your dad who answered the door? He is freaky tall."

He laughed and shook his head. "Oh, no, that's Mr. Vaughn. He works here."

"Then where are your parents? They're never here."

"On business," he said before demanding we change the subject to Izzy and our upcoming science project.

"How did you luck out with her as your partner?"

Michael was right. I was the luckiest boy in the sixth grade. Izzy Winkworth was smart *and* pretty. She wore pretty dresses some days and grass-stained jeans on others. The best part was she wasn't afraid of bugs and she liked swords. Yeah, my luck was finally changing.

Angst of the Middle-school Newbie

~ *19* ~

The rest of sixth grade was moving along smoothly. Vicky Smith was no longer in the bullying business and had even started wearing dresses every now and then. She smiled a lot more and had even been caught being nice, though she would deny it if asked directly.

Michael had good days and bad though he had yet to tell me what was wrong with him. I suppose he will when he's ready. Sometimes he goes weeks without coming to school, and has to catch up on all his work at home. When that happens, Izzy and I hang out with him, and we all do our homework together, while keeping him company. They are my two best friends and, together, we are our own little club. All we need is each other.

Izzy had gone to church with me a few times, even though her parents fought about it a lot. One time, her mom even came, but not her dad. That's okay; we were praying for him, and I know Jesus heard us.

The weeks passed until the day came for us to present our science project. Michael had even talked his dad into donating to help build the garden. Everything was set, and Izzy and I were ready for the big reveal. Tomorrow was the big day. The whole day would be dedicated to science project presentations, and we were the final show.

I barely slept a wink. No amount of counting butterflies or lizards worked. I was too nervous to even close my eyes, so I got down on the floor and looked up at the ceiling.

Dear Jesus, it's me, Philippian Macedon from 222 Carthage Road. Tomorrow is the big day and I am so scared. I have to speak in front of the whole school. I don't think I can do this. You said I don't have to be afraid, but I am. I need You to help me. Please.

And Jesus, could You help Michael Donavan Schmitzer to get better? He's my number one best friend. Please help him, too. He needs You.

Good night Jesus. Please help me go to sleep so I don't mess up tomorrow. I don't want Izzy mad at me again. If You talk to my dad, could You tell him I love him all the way around the world two times and back again? Thank You. Amen.

I crawled into bed and closed my eyes. I don't remember much more after that. I was fast asleep.

The school gathered on the lawn in folded chairs. All the other science projects had been presented, and it was our turn. My throat was so dry I was gulping down my fifth bottle of water when Mrs. Walla motioned for us to take our places in front of the crowd.

The large muscle in the middle of my chest pumped so hard and so fast I was sure my rib-cage would bust open. I wanted to double over and puke. Well, actually, I did.

I stood by Izzy as she told about the many companies that had donated their time and money to fund the butterfly garden. Their money bought plants, soil, concrete tables and benches, and even a white picket fence to keep the garden safe. Others donated their time to help build it ... and everyone helped keep it a secret.

Then it was my turn. I took one last look at my bracelet. *I can do all things through Christ who gives me strength. Philippians 4:13. All things. Even stand in front of a crowd and speak without stuttering. All things.*

The words flowed across my lips like a stream making its way to the ocean. I didn't stutter one time. I told them about the different plants used during each stage of a butterfly's life. I explained the need for at least six hours of direct sunlight, as well as ways to use fruit scraps to attract new butterflies.

Among the many plants we presented were small, shallow saucers filled with wet sand where the butterflies could sip water and bathe, since bird baths are too deep. Most of the school didn't know this.

I explained how they could make their own butterfly gardens in small containers in their backyards. Then I introduced them to Faith-Grace. I explained how she had been injured and how I listened to her clicking noises until I found her. In small groups, everyone was able to walk through the garden and see the butterflies already joining us, as well as the larvae hanging from the dill plant stems.

When it was over, everyone clapped as loud as they could. They even stood and cheered. Izzy and I both got an 'A' for our grade, and received first-place ribbons.

Starting middle school was nothing like I had imagined it would be. I've been working on my *Guide to Surviving Middle School* to hand out to the newbies who will show up next year as afraid as I was.

Summer vacation was just a few days away and, for the first time, I couldn't wait. I had friends to hang out with, and a new baby brother or sister who would be coming in a couple of weeks, which meant my dad would be home soon.

I learned valuable lessons throughout the year. Fear is never something to hold on to, and there is no offense that can't be overcome with peace and kindness. Vicky Smith and I had even become semi-friends. When we passed in the hallway, I jumped as high as I could to smack my hand against hers. Kindness had won. Fear lost.

I was no longer a kid. I was a pre-teen and, in the world of middle school, that made me a man. Since I had already received my bicycle, the only other wish I had for my birthday was to have a real birthday party with actual friends. It was the best birthday ever, except that my dad wasn't there. I'm sure he knows how proud I am that he serves our country, and that I love him all the way around the world two times and back again. He knows. I had holes drilled in the quarters he gave me and turned them into a necklace. I wear it close to my heart so I can feel him there.

Sixth grade had been good to me. I have a feeling seventh grade will be even better, no matter how small I am. I'll get by.

Summer. Ah, summer ... I. Can. Not. Wait! Summer officially begins tomorrow, and I have great things planned. It's going to be the best summer ever. I had been thinking of ideas and designing the world's greatest headquarters for our club. I had it all right up here in my head. Keeping it safe. It's top secret, and only Izzy Winkworth and Michael Donavon Schmitzer will know about it. They will be sworn to silence.

"Tomorrow morning. Don't forget," I reminded my two best friends as I unlocked my bike. "Ten o'clock. Not a minute later!"

"Wait!" Izzy held up one finger. That usually meant she has a great idea to share. "If it is just going to be the three of us, we are going to need a name for our club! That's it. We'll be a club. Just us." She danced in circles, clapping and chanting. "We-are-a-club. We-are-a-club!"

Michael chimed in, "And a secret handshake! Something only the three of us know." He drummed his finger against his forehead and let his tongue hang out of the corner of his mouth. I could practically see his brain spinning. "Just the three of us? Hmmm. We will conquer the world. Protect the neighborhood Right the injustices of the Carthage Road!" He continued thinking.

"Yes! Just the three of us." I was almost ready to hop onto my bike and race the two of them home. Well, at least as far as the three of us would go together before heading off to our own neighborhoods

"We'll come up with a great name. We'll have to earn some money to pay for supplies." She paused for a minute. I could practically see the smoke streaming from her ears with every thought. She held a single finger in the air, which usually meant she had a great idea. "I've got it. We'll have a lemonade stand. I have great lemonade recipes!"

"Yeah!" Michael's smile was so big all his teeth sparkled. "We'll be the Lemonade Brigade."

"Awesome," Izzy and I agreed together. And with that, The Lemonade Brigade strapped on our helmets and headed off into the sunset, ready to start our new journey. Prepared to make our mark on the world.

"Dear Jesus," I prayed right out loud while I peddled and actually kept up with my friends. *"Thank You for getting me through this year and thank You for my two best friends. Oh, and when You talk to my dad, tell him I love him all the way around the world two times and back again. Thank You. Amen."*

It was time to part ways. There we were at the edge of the gravel road that splits off into three different neighborhoods We sat there for a second, excited about the plans we had made.

Michael extended his arm and closed his fist. Izzy did the same. They looked at me and I knew it's what friends in a club do. I balled up my fist and stuck mine in with theirs. We banged them together.

"Lemonade Brigade on three," Michael announced. "One. Two. Three."

All together ... in one voice, we sucked air as much air as we could, all the way from the tips of our toes to the tops of our lungs and shouted, "Lemonade Brigade" and rode off on separate directions.

Until tomorrow...

~ ~ ~

If you are interested in knowing when the next volume in the Philippian 4:13 series is releasing, sign up for the Mr. Row's Adventures newsletter (with your parent's permission at www.MrRowsAdventures.com)

In Volume 2 of the Philippian 4:13 series, Philippian, Izzy, and Michael use their lemonade stand as the headquarters for the crime-solving business. They meet an odd girl named Carie. She quickly becomes part of their team when she is "sentenced" to serving community service with the Lemonade Brigade.

Don't miss this exciting journey.

Volume 2: The Lemonade Brigade. (This will also begin a spin-off series of its own).

You may email the author with any questions or comments @ AuthorKLDierking@gmail.com .

Printed in Great Britain
by Amazon.co.uk, Ltd.,
Marston Gate.